The Good Old Days 1968

ROOKIE COP

MEL LADNER

Brilliant Books Literary
137 Forest Park Lane Thomasville
North Carolina 27360 USA

To all the fine police officers who put their lives on the line every night and day to protect the rights of all of us. God bless you all!

My love, Cindy Schuler, in life Always look for better seats. Thank you for all your help and support and for pointing me in the right direction.

My loving family, Noel & Dan, Dan. S. Guinevere, Cassandra, Juliet, and John Daniel, I love you!

Tom, Fran, Gary, and Alma thank you so much for steering me in the right direction.

My wife Julia of forty-four years who died far too soon. May you rest in peace. I miss and love you.

Please enjoy the book.

INTRODUCTION

Marvin Levey was twenty-one years old. Raised in a Jewish family, he never had a fistfight, a stiff drink, or a serious date with a woman in his life. Marvin's whole life was devoted to reading good books. He became a devoted fan of detective stores and could not put them down. He loved math, excelled in taking tests at school, loved exercising and weightlifting, and being the best son, he could to his mother. That was his life, but he wanted to make a big change.

He needed excitement and adventure in his life, so he decided to become a New York City police officer. He had a lot going for him that made him stand out. He could squeeze into twenty-eight-inch-waist pants with a forty-six chest, sixteen-and -a-half-size arms, a seventeen-inch neck, and a great smile. Marvin could have been a male model. Any woman would be head over heels if asked to out with him, but Marvin had a problem. He was shy and nervous around women. His lack of confidence showed.

Marvin purchased ARCO books to study for the entrance test to the NYC police department. After many hours, he felt he Almost memorized the books.

He read in the New York daily newspaper that there was a walk-in New York City police entrance exam at Jefferson High school that week. He did not tell his mother he was going to take the test.

After he took the test, he had to wait one month for his results. He scored 105 on the test.

"that's not possible," he said.

When he read through the notification letter, he learned that twelve questions had more than one answer. Inside the envelope was a twenty-page investigation form, a phone number, and a return self-stamped envelope. Marvin was supposed to fill those out return them as soon as possible.

He finished in an hour because he had no arrest record or any outstanding summons. Walking down to the corner mailbox, he mailed his form back the same day.

•••••••••••

Three weeks later, Detective Dave Burns called. "I want to congratulate you, Marvin. You passed the investigation. Please report to the Police Academy on April third, 1968, at ten o'clock in the morning. You'll be sworn in that day, you'll receive a certified letter with all details in the next few days. Welcome to the greatest police department in the world!

Marvin, surprised and exited at being accepted, realized the classes began in only two weeks. "Thank you, Detective Burns. I can't wait to join the New York City Police department. I'm looking forward to putting some excitement in my life."

"You'll be incredibly surprised how your life will change once you become a New York City cop. Good luck." He hung up.

•••••••••••

When Marvin Levey went to Lincoln High School in Brooklyn, New York, He was thirteen and had his first encounter with a girl in his class, Ruth. She was also thirteen and was very tall at five-feet-seven inches, with straight, golden-blonde hair and a dazzling mature body. She was the most-beautiful girl in the ninth grade. She could have dated any boy she wanted.

Ruth was madly in love with Marvin and fantasized about him. He loved her, too, but he hadn't the courage to ask her out for a date.

One day, they met accidentally at the local candy store, G.I. Joe is, on Neptune Avenue in their neighborhood. The store was owned by two World War Two veterans and had the place stocked with all the candy and sweet any kid might want. When Marvin walked in, he smelled the sweet and felt right at home.

On the shelves were button candy and log strips of different-colored sugar buttons, Mary Jane bars, loose candy, Halvah, malted milkshakes, egg crème, soda, ice cream with sugar cones and sprinkles, and an ice cream sundae called the Kitchen Sink.

The store Also had an amazing amount of comic books. Some lazy students who did not want to read their assigned books in school bought a classic comic of the story to get the feel of the book instead. Any student could make a good report based on one of those classic comics.

"Hi, Marvin," Ruth said. "I'm so glad you're here." How about we sit down and have a Cherry Coke together? I have something to ask you."

Marvin felt nervous and uncomfortable being with her. "I have to leave."

"Please stay. I want to have a serious talk about our relationship."

He agreed to stay and talk. They sat down and brought their Cherry Coke to the table. Ruth got right to the point.

"I've been thinking about you, Marvin," she said, "for a long time. I hoped you feel the same way I feel about you. I daydream about us being more than just friends,"

Marvin, embarrassed, began shuttering. The situation made him extremely uncomfortable. "What are you saying?"

"I love you, Marvin, "she whispered. "I want you to love me."

Completely shocked, he didn't just know how to handle the situation, but he Also knew he couldn't just say no.

Marvin jumped to his feet and said, "I have to leave now." He ran out the door without taking a sip of his soda or saying good-bye.

He thought about Ruth all the way home. *Am I nuts? I love her. She is a nice, beautiful person. What is wrong with me? I don't want to be a loser throughout my life.*

I need help. I will talk to my mother or maybe my friend Scotto. Maybe they can help me get rid of this. hang-up over women.

Edith, his mother, feared being left alone and would do anything to keep Marvin at home, so she always gave him whatever he wanted.

When he told her what happened, she said?" That girl's crazy and sound like trouble. You should have nothing to do with her or her friends. Remember that you promised your father to take care of me."

Daniel, Marvin's father came from a very wealthy family. At the turn of the nineteenth century, his grandfather invented and patented shoeboxes. The family received royalty payments every three months, enabling them to live comfortably in a middle-class neighborhood.

Daniel worked in the family business and couldn't have been fired even if he wanted to leave. He made a good living and bought a new car every two years, went on vacations, and got a holiday bonus that doubled he annual salary. If he wanted time off, he asked his uncle. It was a good deal for Daniel and his family.

The family looked forward to Marvin's joining the company after he graduated from college.

From then on, whenever Marvin saw Ruth, he avoided her. He never had an encounter with the police and knew nothing about police work. He was a true mommy's boy, frightened of just about everything.

Edith hired Scotto, a weightlifter to stop bullies from picking on Marvin, black belt in Karate, and a tough streetwise kid, to escort Marvin to school to stop bullies from harassing him. Scotto was tough but fair and had a good sense of decency. Though intelligent, he had trouble with math and had to repeat a grade twice in school. He could never lean the basic rules for solving math problems.

Edith. paid Scotto five dollars a week, and he earned every penny of it. Marvin, a frequent target of bullies, didn't know how to defend himself.

Marvin was raised in an upper-middle-class neighborhood in Brooklyn. He went to Lincoln High School on Coney Island, a very tough school that saw fights Almost every day among the students. It was routine to have a bully say, "After school," to someone, meaning he had to fight or run away.

Marvin, the smartest in his class, loved taking tests. He would get angry with himself for missing even one question. The classes were broken down to 9-1, which was the smartest class, while 9-9 was the toughest, where most of the students had learning and behavior problems.

One day Mario Washington, a bully, shoved Marvin and demanded his lunch money. Marvin cried and handed it over. Then Mario said he would meet him before school each day to take his lunch money. Still crying, Marvin agreed.

He told Scotto what happened, and the next day Scotto met Mario where he waited outside the school with a crowd of tough friends to collect Marvin's lunch money. Mario ignored Scotto and demanded his money.

"How about I take the lunch money and shove it up your ass?" Scotto asked.

"You had to bring a friend, "Mario sneered. "That's good. I'll kick his ass, too."

Washington swung at Scotto, which was the biggest mistake of his life. Scotto struck back with an open right hand that shoved Washington's nose Almost up into his forehead. He followed with a left and right to the kid's jaw. He went down hard.

While Mario was semiconscious, Scotto demanded the return of the money he took from Marvin, bleeding furiously, Scotto quickly handed over the money.

Scotto 'At the stunned crowd of Washington's friends, "Any of you idiots want the same? Let's get it on."

They turned away without a comment and helped Washington up.

"Boy, I wish I could do that to bad guys." Marvin said.

"you can," Scotto said. "maybe someday you'll get the chance."

"What can I do to become a winner and get rid of my hang-up when it comes to meeting women?"

The first thing you must do is look the part. You should start lifting weights and getting into shape. You're tall and good-looking. All you need some muscles. Stop being such a wimp. That's a good place to start. Maybe when you get older, you should join the Army or the New York City Police Department. They'll make a man out of you."

Marvin thought about that. "If you could show me how to work out with the weights, maybe you could also show me how to fight."

"I'd be happy to teach you some workouts, but I have to refuse the fighting part. I don't you getting hurt or becoming one of those asses who hang out in the streets and get into trouble. I'll let the Army, or the police department take care of that.

When it comes to meeting women, you just must act the part. Put yourself into one of your favorite movie characters and play the role. With Ruth, you could have played the role of Michael Caine in *Alfie*.

That movie was about a chauffeur who become a womanizer and was extraordinarily successful in his pursuit of women. Whenever you face a situation where you must act your way through it, think of your favorite crowd-pleasing actor and think how he would act his way through the situation to be successful. It works, try it."

"That's a great idea! I'll definitely will play the role of my favorite actors whenever I get into situations where I'm in over my head." From that day on Marvin played the part of one of his favorite actors whenever needed.

•••••••••••

After school, Marvin met Scotto for their walked home. Marvin worried that Washington or his friends would be waiting for them. As they walked home, he kept looking around while they talked.

"I'll talk to my mother if I can have weights in the house so I can work out', Marvin said.

"That's a great idea'.

At home, he asked Edith, and she said, "weights will make you muscle bound. You will not have full range of motion with your arms. That's crazy."

Marvin started crying. "I want the weights, and I want to work out so I can become a cop."

"No way will you become a cop. It's too dangerous. You have a nice job waiting, working for your uncle in the shoebox business. If you promise to get that crazy idea of becoming a cop out of your head, we will try the weights. If those weights and work-out don't work, I'll throw you and your weights out of the house!"

Marvin went to the Yellow Pages and found a sports store called Joe Wielder. He dialed the number on the rotary phone.

"May I help you?" the clerk asked.

"I'm looking for a starter set of weights. How much would that cost?"

"We have a 110-pound set that comes with two dumbbells that sells for $14.99. if we must deliver it, the cost is $25.00."

'I'll pick them up. Where are you located?'

"We're at Fulton Street in downtown Brooklyn."

"That's a train ride. I'll have to take the Clove line. I'll be there after school tomorrow."

"See you then."

"Marvin hung up and went to ask Edith for the money for the weights."

She said, "If you want to become a muscle-bound freak, you have to use your own money."

"If I get big and strong from working-out, that will save you money. I'll be able to go to school Alone and defend myself from bullies.

"I don't want you fighting."

Marvin cried again, and she gave in like usual. She handed him the money.

············

Marvin met Scotto at his house and walked toward school.

"How do I work out with weights?" Marvin asked.

"The basic principle is that you want to tear down muscles have the muscles heal. When they do that, they become stronger and larger. It's simple. You just do three sets and thirteen repetitions for each part of the body. Pretty simple, huh?"

Marvin's weights were the beginning of having a full gym in his house. Marvin and Scotto became good friends and worked out five days a week together.

"Can you help me with my math homework?" Scotto asked one day.

"Sure. I can teach you how to solve most math problems. Can you help me overcome my shyness around girls?"

"That's a lot harder than doing math."

They both laughed.

CHAPTER ONE

Rookie Cop!

What would you do if you had only one day as a New York City police officer and were thrown onto the streets to quell riots, make arrests, and fight for your life without any training? The April 3, 1968 class at the Academy had the distinction of being the only Police Academy class in the history of New York City never to graduate from the Academy.

. . . .

Marvin Levey was ordered to report to the Police Academy at 235 East Twentieth Street in Manhattan at 0800 hours wearing a business suit and to bring ten cents. It was traditional that new recruits had to pay ten cents for the safety pin that held their police shield onto their uniform, though the shield itself was free.

The tradition went back to 1624, when the city was founded when police officers were called watchmen. The old night watchman system was replaced in 1857 with the municipal police force that grew into the New York City Police Department.

The recruits lined up in the gymnasium and approached a long lunch table, where the academy gym instructors handed out new police shields with the number that would stay with each recruit for
of his career.

The instructors gave Marvin a piece of paper with his tax registry number, an important document used for seniority. Seniority determined an officer's vacation time, promotions, assignments, and retirement. He was told to report on April 5, 1968 to the Police Academy at 0800 hours for roll call on the muster deck on the roof of the building, where all rookie cops reported at start of their tour of duty.

Not all candidates who were ordered to appear would be appointed to the Police Department. The city budget dictated the exact who would be hired to fill the department ranks.

Marvin was on the list that made the class. After he received, his shield and orders, he felt his whole life change. Suddenly, he had more friends than he could imagine-over 30,000 police officers just in New York City. Worldwide, over 5 million law-enforcement officers would be willing to help him. All he had to do was identify himself as a member of the New York City Police Department, and the other officers would extend him professional courtesy.

After receiving his shield and orders, Marvin sat in the police academy gym with 1,521 other recruits, and the ceremony began.

First, New York Mayor John Lindsay, who was elected in 1965, gave a ten-minute speech thanking them for joining. He was Yale law graduate and a good-looking man. He told the recruits that police work was more than arresting criminals. It meant helping people, delivering babies, saving lives, helping people that are sick or injured, and protecting the weak and disadvantage.

When he finished, the audience gave him a standing ovation.

Chief of Patrol Stan Cohen, the highest-ranking officer in the department, spoke "Look to your right. Now look to your left. In the next twenty years of your police career, one of you will be fired, injured in the line of duty, or in jail for doing something stupid. That's what our statistics show.

"I received a letter from Mrs. Julia Ladner, the wife of Mel Ladner, a recruit and member of this class, and I'd like to read you a portion of the letter. She titled it *What Is a Cop?*"

Cops are human. They're just like

of us. They come in both sexes but are mostly males. They Also come in various sizes. This sometimes depends on whether you're looking for one or hiding from one.

Cops are found everywhere: on land, in the air, on horses, in cars, and sometimes in your hair. Despite the fact that you can't find one when you want one, they're usually there when it counts. The best way to get one is to pick up the phone and ask for one.

Cops deliver lectures, babies, and bad news. They're required to have the wisdom of Solomon, the disposition of a lamb, and muscles of steel. Cops ring doorbells, swallow hard, and announce the passing of a loved one, then they spend

of the tour wondering why they took such a job.

On TV, a cop is an oaf who couldn't find a bass fiddle in a phone booth. In real life, he's expected to find a little blond boy about so high in a crowd of half a million people. In fiction, he's helped by private eyes, reporters, and whodunit fans. In real life, mostly all he gets from the public is, "I didn't see nothing."

When he serves a summons, he's a devil. If he lets you go, he's an angel. To little kids, he's either a friend or a bogeyman, depending on how the parents feel about cops. He works around the clock, split shifts, Sundays, and holidays, and it always kills him when a joker asks, "Hey, tomorrow's election day. Let's go fishing", when he knows he's working twenty-four-hour shift.

A cop is like the little girl, who, when she was good, was very, very good, but when she was bad, she was horrid. When a cop is good, he's getting paid for it. When he makes a mistake, he's a grafter, and that goes for

of them, too. When he shoots a stick-up man, he's a hero, except when the stick-up man is only a kid with a toy gun that looks real, and you've got only a fraction of a second to make a decision if you're going home that night. Then the public comes out and Sunday quarterbacks your decision and concludes that the cop is wrong, and anybody could see it was a toy gun.

Lots of cops have homes, some of them covered in ivy, but most are covered with large mortgages. If he drives a big car, he's chiseler. If he owns an old, little car, who's he kidding? His credit is good. This is extremely helpful because his salary isn't. Cops raise lots of kids, most of them belonging to other people.

A cop sees more misery, bloodshed, trouble, and sunrises than the average person. Like the postman, cops must be in all kinds of weather. His uniform changes with the climate, but his outlook on life remains about the same, hoping for a better world.

Cops like days off, vacations, and coffee. They don't like auto horns, family fights, and characters who write anonymous letters. They must be impartial, courteous, and Always remember the slogan, *At your service.* This is sometimes hard, especially when a character reminds him, he's a taxpayer and says, "I pay your salary."

Cops get medals. Sometimes, his widow gets the medal for saving lives, stopping runaway horses, and shooting it out with bandits. Sometimes, the most-rewarding moment comes when after some small kindness from an older person, he feels a warm handclasp, looks into grateful eyes, and hears, "Thank you, and God bless you Son."

• • • • • • • • • • • •

Chief Cohen stopped to look at the class. There was stunned silence. He continued.

After you leave the Police Academy, all you police officers will know what the job is all about.

Read the orders. I don't want any recruits to come in tomorrow. You have the day off.

The Patrolman's Benevolent Association delegate will have you sign a check-off form that will automatically deduct your union dues from your paycheck. You have no choice. You must join the PBA. That is our policy.

This is the time to notify your employer if you haven't done so that you're now a member of the greatest police department in the world, the New York City Police Department. Enjoy the day with your family.

"Be safe, and God bless you and your family." Chief Cohen looked at them for a moment. "Stand up and raise your right hand."

Chief Clerk of the city of New York Louis Studman issued the oath of office.

Probationary Police Officer Marvin Levey was appointed and sworn into the New York Police Department on April 3, 1968, at noon with 1,521 other probationary police officers. The class of April 3, 1968 was so large, it had to be split into two sessions. One met from 8;00 AM to 4:00 PM. The other met from 4:00 PM to midnight. The class was down to companies, with number sixty-eight standing for the year. The class that began in February 1968 had eighteen companies, so the April class of that year started with company 68-19. Each company held thirty to thirty-six recruits.

It was the largest class in the history of the New York City Police Department.

Marvin was assigned to company 68-19, which meant it ran from 8:00 AM to 4:00 PM. Starting on April 5, 1968, his first full day as a New York City Probationary Police Officer.

After being sworn in, Marvin met his fellow recruits and started looking for others who belonged to his company to form a study group. He assumed learning all the laws and regulations would be difficult. He found two other members and quickly introduced himself.

"I'm Jim Healy, one said. "Boy, am I lucky to make this class. Somebody must've failed to show up. I was in the group that was notified in case someone didn't show. Now I have to tell my boss at the liquor store that I'm history."

"Hi, I'm Pete Cahill glad to meet fellow member of our class 68-19", the other young man said. "This was some day. It'll make my grandfather and father proud of me. They were both cops. It's all they talk about. Both retired a long time ago.

"Let me warn you about some of the rules of this game. Don't tell any of your neighbors that you're a cop. In fact, it's better no one knows."

"why?" Marvin asked.

"You don't want them dropping a dime on you."

Marvin was puzzled.

"You don't want them to complain about you, especially during your six months' probation. You could lose this job for Almost anything during that time. After that, they'll have to shoot you to get rid of you. Looks like you guys don't know shit about police work."

Pete continued explaining what he learned about being a cop during his childhood. "One other thing before I forget. Go to the back of the Academy through the Thirteenth Precinct across Twenty-First Street. There's a police department store there. Buy a shield wallet with a chain that'll attach to your belt. It's the best investment you can make."

"Why's that?" Marvin asked.

"God forbid you lose that shield. It'll cost you thirty days' pay, and you'll be suspended. When you're on probation and you lose the police shield it's very serious offense, you're police career is finished."

"Whoa!"

"let's go there right now," Jim said, in a panic.

"Don't worry. We won't lose our shields," Pete added. "There's a way to protect ourselves from that. Next week, we'll go to a store in Flatbush that'll make a DUP shield that's an eighth inch smaller than the original police shield. No one can tell the difference. Just in case".

"I think you've got a real future in police work," Jim said.

"This is all new to me," Marvin said.

"Me, too," Jim said.

"Don't worry. It's pretty simple. It's called CYA, cover your ass. There are some other rules of the game. We'll get into those over drinks. Maybe we can meet tomorrow and get out shit together."

They agreed to meet for drinks and dinner at six o'clock at Farrell's Bar at the circle by Prospect Park, Brooklyn.

"Where do you guys live?" Marvin asked.

"Brooklyn," Pete said.

"We should start a study group."

"Are you kidding that's the last thing on my mind?" Jim asked. "I'm thinking about a good, stiff drink."

"That sounds like a good idea," Pete said. "I could go for a drink, too."

Pete and Jim lived in Brooklyn. They exchanged numbers with each other and promised to call once they were home.

Marvin went to his mother, who witnessed the ceremony. "I have to go to the police store before I go home, I need a shield case and chain."

When they went through the Thirteenth Precinct, the desk sergeant asked, "What is this Grand Central Station? Can I help you?"

He was in his sixties, pale as a ghost complexion, a bald head, an overweight body, and with a slight Irish brogue when he spoke.

"No, thanks," Marvin said, "we're going to the police store and just passing through."

"Come over here, son. Are you on the job?"

"Yes, Sir. I was sworn in about thirty minutes ago."

"Let me see your shield."

Marvin showed him the shield, and the sergeant studied it. "Looks like they'll take anybody these days. Son let this be a warning to you. Never, ever, come into a police station unless you have police business. The less we see of you, the better off you are, and we are. Got it?"

"Yes, Sir."

"No. You call me Sergeant."

Marvin and his mother Almost ran out of the building.

"Are you sure you want to do police work?" she asked.

"I don't know. I'll give it a chance. If it doesn't work out, I can always sell shoeboxes."

Edith laughed.

The police store was crowded with new recruits buying everything in sight.

"Marvin, you can buy whatever you want," Edith said. "I'll pay for it."

The Salesclerk came over. He was a retired detective and a gunsmith. "what can I get you, Officer?"

Marvin turned toward the man. "I just became a police officer. What do you think I need for police work?"

"You don't need much while you're at the academy. When you get to the streets, it's a different story."

"So, I don't have to come in again, let's get the stuff now. Show me your top-notch stuff."

The clerk nodded, showing his understanding that money was no object. "OK."

"What's the best shield wallet you have?"

"You got it. Don't you want to know what the costs is?"

"I trust you. I know you won't rob me. What about an off-duty holster?"

"You won't be issued a gun or at least four months."

"What kind of gun will it be?"

"Most likely a six-shot Smith and Wesson service revolver. You might want some 158-gram hollow point ammo, too."

"Sure."

"A box?"

"Yeah. How may bullets come in a box?"

"Fifty rounds."

Marvin Also bought an off -duty holster for his service revolver.

"What about a nightstick? The one the department issues you is so light; you couldn't harm a fly with it. I recommend the Cocobolo nightstick. It's made out of very hardwood. One hit on the head, and the bad guy will be talking Japanese."

"I'll take it."

"While I'm thinking about it, you might as well get a blackjack, called a slapper." He got one out and showed Marvin how it worked. "You want to hit the perp with the flat part of the blackjack. If you hit him with the edge of the jack, you'll have blood all over you and your uniform, and those uniform aren't cheap. All you must do is swing it and hit the perp's on his head once. That'll end the fight and you will go home safe and sound.

"When you get good at police work, you can hide it in your glove. If you want to arrest some idiot, just stomp hard on his foot and he'll automatically push you. Then you can whack him with your glove and arrest him. Believe me, it works. You can do that trick in the middle of a crowd, and nobody will know what happened. The slapper's flat and has a spring on the handle. It's about six-inches long with a black, enclosed hard leather cover with the end of the blackjack holding four ounces of lead."

"What else do I need?"

"You won't see the street for at least four months. You'll be stuck in the police academy for that time.

"I might as well get what I want now. Why wait? You never know."

"Just one more thing. Insert a list of code of the traffic laws and penal laws for your memo book."

"What's a memo book?"

The clerk laughed. "You don't know shit about what you're getting yourself into, I wish my mother were like yours. She's treating you like it's Christmas."

"We're Jewish! Edith said.

"There aren't many Jewish cops on the job. They're all bosses."

Marvin and Edith left the police store and walked from Second Avenue and Twenty-First to the Twenty-Third Street subway station on Lexington Avenue. Marvin carried two large shopping bags full of new police equipment. When they arrived, he saw a large crowd of recruits using their shields to go through the gate for free.

Marvin went to the subway clerk. "Do I have to pay the fare if I'm a cop?"

"Absolutely not. Just show your badge on any subway or bus, and you get on for nothing. That is part of your benefits. Your mother can ride for free with you, too."

"Thanks." Showing the subway clerk his shield, he went through the gate with Edith before boarding the train, wondering what other benefits he might have.

On the train home, he and Edith talked.

"Mom, please don't tell anyone in the neighborhood I'm a cop."

"Why not?"

He explained what Pete Cahill said. Edith agreed not to tell anyone in the neighborhood, though she was immensely proud that her son was a cop. She decided she could tell her family.

•••••••••••

Once they were home, Marvin called Thomas Scotto at he the New York Stock Exchange, where he worked as a floor page.

"I just became a New York City Police Officer," Marvin said.

"That's great. Now if I get into trouble, I'll have someone to call to get me out of a jam."

They laughed.

"I have to go. The stock market's crazy today we have over a three-million stocks trading today, and I'm really busy. I'll call you after I'm off work at three-thirty."

Marvin hung up, then he called Jim and Pete. They agreed to meet at Farrell's Bar and Grill at the park circle at six o'clock next day, April 4,1968.

．．．．．．．．．．．．

Marvin arrived early. The bar was a landmark, a real drinking man's bar. It opened in 1933 in what a tough Irish neighborhood was then. Beer was served in Styrofoam cups. The TV was loud and showed *Hawaii Five -O* starring Jack Lord, playing Detective Steve McGarrett. The volume was so high, the words were unintelligible. The background noise in the bar was deafening. Cigarette and cigar smoke were so thick you could cut the smoke with a knife.

Farrell's Bar didn't serve unchaperoned women until Shirley MacLaine, the actress insisted on being served there. The bar than served single women ever since.

Marvin felt uncomfortable at Farrell's bar, because it was his first-time he went to bar in his life. The bartender came over.

"What do you want?"

Marvin looked at him. "I'm waiting for two friends I'm meeting here. I'll have coffee with milk and sugar."

"Who are your friends?"

"Pete Cahill and Jim Healy."

"I know Pete very well. He's here all the time. He said he recently became a cop. Are you a cop, too?"

Marvin didn't know what to say. "May I have the coffee now?"

The bartender walked away to prepare a cup of coffee for him.

Pete showed up, and he hugged Marvin. The bartender returned with Marvin's coffee and a cup of milk.

Pete looked at Marvin. "This is a bar. You know they serve drinks here."

"I don't drink, and this is the first time I ever been too a bar. "Marvin felt embarrassed.

"You're a cop now, and most cops are Irish. That's the culture of the NYCPD. If you want to fit in, you have to start drinking, even just a little. I don't mean wine, either. Nobody trusts a person who won't

drink and go to bars. All the people I ever met who didn't drink all had something wrong with them.

Jim Healy came in and greeted Pete and Marvin like they won the lottery.

The bartender came over. "Pete, what do you guys want?"

"Before we order, I'd like to introduce my fellow New York City Police Officers, Jim and Marvin Levey. Remember to take care of them."

"You're entitled to a NYCPD discount on food and drinks. Marvin, that includes coffee, the bartender said.

Pete and Jim ordered three stiff drinks and the special dinner of the day. Marvin order a tuna fish sandwich with French dressing and Cole slaw on the side.

"Who's the third drink for?" Marvin asked.

"You, "Pete said. "You're a cop now. Don't embarrass us in the bar."

Marvin considered that for a minute. "What the hell. It can't hurt to have one drink. OK. You talked me into it. I'll have that drink."

Marvin told them the story of trying to cut through the Thirteenth Precinct.

"CYA," Pete said, cutting him off. "Cover your ass. I told you that. You should have had a story ready, like the captain forgot his car keys and were taking them to him. The sergeant would never call the captain to ask about it. Got that, Marvin? Always have a story to cover your ass."

The drinks came, and they were toasting each other, when suddenly, someone screamed at the bar.

"Holly shit!" someone shouted. "They killed King!"

All eyes went to the TV, which was tuned to ABC news, Tom Jarriel reported the Reverend Martin Luther King Jr. had just been assassinated.

That brought back memories of President John F. Kennedy's assassination.

Jim, Pete, and Marvin looked at each other and then ran over to the TV set. They and the large bar crowd watched in shock of the news that Dr. Martin Luther King; Jr. was killed.

"Let's go back to our table and have that drink."

"I need one, too, "Marvin said. He downed it in one gulp.

"You sure you never had a drink before?" Pete asked. "they all laughed."

"What now?" Marvin asked.

"Maybe we should go to the Academy," Jim said.

"Sit tight. The job will call you if you're need. We'd be the last people in the world they'd want to use. If they put us in the streets, that means the city's in deep shit."

They stared at the TV and saw riots had already begun in the city.

"Holly shit, Jim said. "Looks at the riots starting everywhere in the country. You know we'll get them here, too."

The others nodded.

"What do we do" Marvin asked.

"Let's have another drink and bring our food closer to the TV," Pete said. "We'll finish our meals and get the hell out of her. We will go home and wait for a call from the job. That sound like a plan."

They finished their drinks and food.

The bartender came over. "Drinks, dinner, and coffee are on the arm. I wish you guys the best of luck. You'll need it. This city is ready to explode."

As they left, Marvin asked, "What does on the arm mean?"

"It's for free," Pete explained. "That's police talk. My grandfather Mike O'MAlley told me a police story back in 1941. He began walking a beat in Brooklyn's Twenty-First Precinct and was taken out to lunch by his partner, a senior officer.

"The meal was probably only a half-buck in those days. The bill came, and the officer who invited him said, "Kid, this isn't a freebie. We pay by leaving a big tip for the waitress. Grandfather learned that many restaurants offered police meals for free, or on the arm.

"He grandfather Also recalled a cashier at another restaurant on Fulton Street. When my grandfather was about to pay his bill, he was in a long line. The cashier took his five dollars and handed him back five singles in change. "the meals are on the arm," he said. People in line didn't know what that meant, but my grandfather did."

They walked outside of Farrell's bar and looked at each other with a mixture of excitement, anxiety, and the feeling they would be needed. Would it get so bad that the department would put rookies on the streets before their four months training ended?

As they walked around Prospect Park, they heard fire and police department sirens constantly in the background on all sides. Smoke rose from the east side of the park, in Crown Heights, Brooklyn.

"Let's get the hell out of here, Pete said.

Going toward their separate homes, they agreed to call each other if they had any news.

"We'll meet tomorrow at the restaurant on First Avenue and Twentieth Street, Marvin said," around seven AM."

"See you tomorrow," Pete and Jim said.

It was ten o'clock that evening, and Marvin needed to take the train to Coney Island that came from Manhattan. He noticed there were no cops anywhere. Probably were tied up working the riots.

When he boarded his train, heard screams and loud curses from inside the train. Ten black teenagers were beating and kicking a white, middle-age man in a business suit, robbing him. The man is cover with blood and screaming in excruciating pain begging for the robbers to stop beating and robbing him! As the train door opened, the passengers fleeing for their lives could not seem to leave the train fast enough.

Marvin held the door open to let them all escape. When four construction workers with tool bags came running by, one stopped and asked his buddies, "What are we running for? Let's go back in and help that poor guy."

Without thinking, Marvin said "I'm a cop."

"All we need is your authorization, and we'll hand what's left of them over to you. You can arrest what's left of them."

"You got it."

"Watch our bags," one construction worker said, as he put down his tool bag on the train station floor in front of Marvin.

The four construction workers pulled out sledge hammers and crowbars and told the teenagers to stop. When they did not stop beating the man. The four construction workers kicked the living shit out of the gang of robbers. Blood was everywhere. The robbery victim crawled out the open train doors and stopped between the doors and the train platform, covered in blood and barely conscious.

Marvin ran to the man and realized he did not know what to do. "Holly shit."

He looked inside the train and saw the robbers laying in a pool of blood on the train floor. When the construction workers ran over to Marvin, they looked at the victim.

"He looks in bad shape," one construction worker said. "Do you know CPR?"

"I need help," Marvin said. "Can you guys call the police to come down and help me?"

"We're leaving. We'll call the police and an ambulance for you."

The construction men grabbed their tool bags and ran and exited the train station.

Marvin "thanked the men just before they left." Without taking any names, he watched them go. Marvin was left with the victim and robbers all Alone.

In a matter of minutes, a train crew ran up and offered aid to all the injured.

"What happened here?" The train conductor asked.

"I'm a cop," Marvin said. "there was a robbery on the train, and we stopped it. The people in the train on the floor are the ones who committed the robbery. The man on the train station floor is the victim."

"Got it."

The construction workers called in a 10-13, which meant officer in trouble. Every police car in the area raced to the train station and arrive almost simultaneously. In seconds, Marvin saw a captain, one lieutenant, two sergeants, and ten regular police officers.

The officers stared in shock at the ten robbers lying in the train car in excruciating pain and unconscious in pools of their own blood. And the victim laying on the platform floor next to Marvin semiconscious and barely breathing.

"You kicked the shit out of them all by yourself?" one officer asked.

Marvin remembered Pete's warning about CYA. Since no one else was on the scene but the train crew who came latter and did not see what happen, he decided he might as well take the credit for what the construction workers did.

"Yes, I did," he said nervously.

The captain stared at him long and hard. "What's your name, Officer?"

"Marvin Levey?"

"Are you Jewish?"

He hesitated, wondering why the officer asked such a question. "Yes, I am."

How many years have you been on the job?"

Marvin laughed. "You won't believe this, but I have about twenty-three hours on the job. I was sworn in yesterday."

The captain studied the ten unconscious bodies, while medics worked to keep some of them Alive. "Are you hurt? Do you have a gun yet?"

"No, I'm not hurt. I'm unarmed."

"Marvin, you're a Super Jew. We'll definitely need officers like you in the city to keep this place safe. I'll call your command at the Academy and see if we can get you a medal for this arrest."

"Is this my arrest?"

"Yes. Don't worry. You have the victim as a complainant witness and I'll assign an experienced officer to process the arrest for you, so you won't miss anything at the Academy.

"Give the information about this event and your shield number to the sergeant, and we'll let you go home. You'll hear from us when you have to appear in court for this case. We'll sent the information to your command, too. You really are a Super Jew."

From that time on, Marvin's nickname in the police department was Super Jew.

Marvin rode home on the subway, wondering, *What the hell did I just do?* He thought about the gruesome scene he left behind and all the people who'd been hurt. *Why didn't I get the names of those construction workers?*

He came up with a plan. First, he couldn't tell his mother. She'd kill him if she found out what happened.

Second, he had to stick with his story. If he tried to change it, his superiors would come down on him hard. He could claim he had a blackjack with him that he used on the robbers.

Marvin arrived home at two-thirty on the morning of April 5, 1968.

Edith met him at the door. "How was your day?"

He laughed. "It was just another day, Mom."

"You should see the news. There were riots all over. They had a riot on the subway train you usually take. Ten muggers were arrested, and the victim died. By the way, Scotto called. He said he'd call back tomorrow. He's tied up with something important on the Stock Exchange and is terribly busy."

"Did they describe the victim?"

"He was forty-three, marred, and had two kids. He worked as a teller for the Lincoln Savings bank. I believe his name was Harry, but I didn't get his last name. one other thing-they said it was a rookie cop who subdued all ten robbers and arrested them. They wouldn't give the rookie's name, but they called him Super Jew. I'll bet that rookie's in your Police Academy class."

Marvin bit his tongue to keep from telling the truth. "I have to get up early tomorrow to meet my new friends at the academy."

The phone rang, and Marvin answered quickly. "Hello?"

"This is Detective Blake Lanier of the homicide squad. Levey, I heard you did a great job a couple hours ago. I just wanted to touch base with you. The victim died of knife wounds. It seems he tried to defend himself and was stabbed in the right armpit. When the victim raised his arm, you couldn't see the puncture wound without taking off his shirt. He bled to death. You did a great job, and the whole department's proud of you."

"What was the man's name? can you tell me where he lived or anything else about him?"

"Let me look at the UF61 and the DD5. That's the investigation form we use Hmmm. His name's Harry Bernstein, he lived near you on 2816 Courtland Street, apartment C-6. That is about six blocks from your house. My partner notified and interviewed the wife, Miriam. They have two young children, three years old and one year old. Harry had two jobs and was coming home from his second one when he was murdered by those skels. I wish I'd been there to see you kick the shit out of those animals.

"What's next?"

"We got in touch with the Brooklyn District Attorney's office. The ten skels are Already turning on each other and seem ready to plead guilty to a lesser charge. Most likely, you won't have to testify. I've been on this job for twenty-three year, and I never saw what you did to those skels. The captain said they call you Super Jew, and boy, they're right.

"Get a good night's sleep, and don't worry. We're here to help, not hurt you. We'll write this up. The captain already said he'd sigh off on the recommendation for the combat cross medal, since the perps were armed. You might not realize this but you're starting to become a legend at NYCPD. Not bad for your first day on the job."

"Thanks. I don't know what to say."

"Good night, Super Jew." He hung up.

"What was that about?" Edith asked.

"I wasn't going to tell you until tomorrow. I was the rookie cop on that train. I arrested those ten murderers."

"What? Are you crazy? You could've been killed!"

"That's my job. We'll talk about it tomorrow."

"You're changing before my eyes. They don't pay you enough for doing this job. It's too dangerous. You should quit."

"I have to get up early tomorrow. Good night." He hugged her and kissed her cheek. "I love you, Ma. I'll Always be here for you."

He went to his room. Though he was tired, he couldn't sleep and kept thinking over and over what happened. *I'm really changing, but maybe that's for the better,* the thought.

April 5,1968
Let's Start the Police Academy

•••••••••••

Marvin woke at five o'clock that morning to an alarm clock radio tuned to 1010 WINS, New York, a station with twenty-four-hour news, weather, and traffic reports. Their slogan was, "You give us twenty-two minutes, and we'll give you all the news." The station never played music and was the first all-news station in the country.

The news was bad. Reverend Martin Luther King Jr. a great civil rights leader and Nobel Peace Prize laureate, had been assassinated. He was known as the leader of nonviolent disobedience marches and nonviolent demonstrations. He was only thirty-nine the day he was killed on April

4, 1968, at 6:01 PM Central Standard Time at the Lorraine Motel in Memphis, Tennessee. He was pronounced dead at St. Joseph's Hospital at 7:05 PM. The riots broke out across America when it was announced that the Reverend Martin Luther King Jr. was shot.

Many states, along with the federal government, declared a state of emergency and called up the National Guard, but the riots continued. There were 102 U.S. cities with uncontrolled riots in progress. Those reporting the most damage was New York City, Washington, Baltimore, Louisville, Kansas City, Chicago, Detroit, Wilmington, Delaware, and Newark, N.J. Hundreds of people were killed or injured during the riots.

A crowd of 20,000 rioters overwhelmed the police force in Washington, DC, which had only 3,100 police officers. President Lyndon B. Johnson called up 13,600 federal troops, including 1,750 National Guard, to try to quell the riots to no avail. They needed more help.

Army troops from the Third Infantry manned machine guns on the steps of the Capitol and guarded the White House.

Washington, D.C. imposed a curfew and banned the sale of Alcohol and guns in the city.

By the time the city was considered safe on Sunday, April 28, 1968, 1200 buildings had been burned, including over 900 stores. The damages were estimated at $320 million dollars. Hundreds were killed or injured. The city of Washington, DC, sustained the worst damage it had seen since the Civil war.

James Earl Ray who shot Dr. Martin Luther King Jr. with a Remington Model 760 Gamemaster 30.06 sniper rifle was a fugitive from Missouri prison who was arrested at Heathrow in London on June 8, 1968 on a fugitive warrant. He pleaded guilty and was sentenced to ninety-nine years in prison.

In New York City, policemen were beaten to death by rioters. Civilian were beaten robbed shot and stabbed. The rioters took over trains and beat and robbed the passengers. Gimbels Department Stores, E.J. Korvette's Department Stores, and other businesses were burned to the ground. Fires and the smell and clouds of heavy thick smoke appeared in some of the Wealthiest neighborhoods in the city.

Marvin listening to the news, thought, *this isn't a normal day. What's in store for me? There's no way this day can top yesterday, though.*

He put on his best suit, with shiny block shoes and black socks, and ran out the door. He had to take the same train he used the previous evening, the Clover Line, and hoped there would not be any trouble.

He made it to Twenty-third and Lexington without incident. The train was filled with men his age, all wearing suits. With that many recruits on board, it felt like the safest train in the city.

Marvin overheard someone discussing the arrest he made on the train. He explained he was the one who did it. The other recruits, staring in amazement, congratulated him like he was a rock star. Marvin carefully left out how he subdued them All.

"How'd you do it?" someone asked.

"The homicide detective in charge told me not of go into any detail," Marvin said. *I'm getting good at CYA.*

He walked east on Twenty-third toward the police academy on Twentieth Street with a large crowd of recruits.

At the academy, they saw twenty city buses double-parked in front, the drivers sitting in their seats. Marvin knocked on a bus door, and the driver opened the bus door.

"What's going on?"

"I figured you must be a cop," the driver replied. "We were asked to work overtime and bring our buses to the Academy. I don't have a clue beyond that."

Marvin left the other recruits at the Academy entrance and went to the restaurant. On the walls were photos of past and present police heroes. He was Detective Lieutenant Mario Biaggi who became a U.S. Congressman, Chief Inspector Sanford Garelik, the first Jewish chief inspector in New York City Police Department, and a city councilman, Irma Lozada, the first female police officer to die in the line of duty, and Police Commander Lloyd Sealy, the first African-American New York City Police Commander in the department's history. As he stared at all the pictures of past heroes and read about the history of the department, he thought, *it's an honor to have your picture on this wall.*

Pete and Jim sat at a table where an empty chair waited for him.

"I'm glad you're here," Marvin said. "Boy, do I have a story for you. I need some help."

"Slow down, Marvin, "Pete said. "Let's say hello first. What are all those buses doing outside the Academy?"

"I asked the driver," Marvin said, "They don't know, either. I'll bet money it has something to do with the riots in the city."

"They can't throw us into the streets without any training," Pete said. "It makes no sense."

"There's no way we'll be out there stopping the riots, "Jim added. "What were you going to say?"

"Did you hear about the rookie who arrested ten murderers yesterday evening on the train?"

"Yes. Do you mean it was you?"

"Yes, but there's more to it. You must agree not to tell anyone what I'm going to say. Promise me and swear to God."

"Whatever you tell us will be a secret," Pete said, "From now on, whatever we tell each other will be confidential."

"I agree, Jim said.

Marvin explained the details of the arrests. "All I did was hold open the train door and let those construction workers kick the living shit out of those murderers."

Pete laughed. "This is a perfect storm, Marvin. You must stick to your story. Nobody wants to hang you, but don't ever give them enough rope to hang you, either. If you play your cards right, you'll be company sergeant soon, and anyone who was involved in the arrest will be promoted. Why would they come after you? You're in the catbird seat. Even the district attorney gets a commendation letter from the mayor for an outstanding job done. Everyone wins if you succeed."

Jim and Marvin nodded.

"Now you have to play the role of a real police hero," Pete continued, "You have to act the part of a cool cop. First, you must become a ladies' man. You must drink at police events, and, more importantly, act tough. If you can pull that off, you'll be a first-grade detective in no time."

They all knew that first-grade detectives were appointed by the police commissioner and received a lieutenant's pay.

"It looks like the only thing you didn't do was get laid," Jim said.

"I would have, but I was too tied up after holding the train door open for three minutes."

They laughed.

"Watch me get cool. I don't think it's that hard to do. I'll try my Paul Newman impression right now."

Pete and Jim looked at him, then shook their heads.

"I think we just created a Frankenstein," Pete said.

"OK, Marvin," Jim said, "How will you start being cool?"

"First, my name isn't Marvin anymore. Its Super Jew." He turned toward the waitress and called out in a very loud voice. "How about some service here!" We've been waiting."

The waitress stopped work and came over to their table. Her name tag read *Flo*. She loved cops and was thirty-five, divorced three times to three different cops. She had three kids and had to work to support them, at five-feet-five-inches tall, she was an attractive thin woman with large breasts and a heavy Brooklyn accent.

"Sorry," she said. "I was busy."

"I want to introduce ourselves to you, because we'll be in here at seven o'clock every morning, Monday to Friday for the next four months," Marvin said, "This is Jim, and this is Pete. I'm Super Jew. If you can have a table reserved and coffee ready for us every Monday through Friday, we'll take care of you.

"Are you the guy they're calling Super Jew? Your name is all over the news!"

"Yes, I am."

"Can we get a picture with your autograph to hang on the our wall with the other police heroes?"

"Sure. If you reserve a table for us every weekday morning, that would be great. Flo said,

The boss and Flo came back with a Nikon 35mm camera and took Marvin's picture.

"You're cute, Super Jew," Flo said. "Here's my phone number. Maybe we can hook up this weekend when your off duty. What do you say?"

I must be cool in front of my friends, Marvin thought, standing and putting his arm around her waist and pulling her tightly against his body for a kiss with plenty of tongue in front of everyone. "That's your tip, he said, as all the people in the coffee shop stood up and applauded and cheered "Super Jew! Super Jew!" in unison.

"I look forward to our first date, Super Jew."

"Super Jew, you have a table here anytime you want it," the boss said.

Pete and Jim stared in amazement.

"Marvin, you're some piece of work, Jim said.

"You make me proud, Marvin," Pete added. "If you keep that up, you'll be a superstar not only in the department but in the real world, too.

They ate as quickly as they could and paid their bill. Marvin stopped by Flo as they left.

"I'll call you. We can get together this weekend, I promise," he said.

"How about I call you?"

He gave her his home phone number and left for the Academy. They walked fast past the double-parked buses.

"I think we're going somewhere on those buses, Pete said.

"No way, Jim said. "We have no training."

The department needs help to stop the rioters. Where would they get more manpower?"

Other officers were working thirty-six hours straight with only a two-hour break between twelve-hour shifts. That meant it was definite that the rookies would be needed to stop the riots.

IN AND OUT OF THE ACADEMY IN ONE DAY

The muster deck was on the roof of the Academy, and that was where the rookies met each morning. They saw smoke billowing from Brooklyn to the east and Harlem to the north. All around came the constant sound of sirens from the police and fire departments emergency vehicles responding to calls for help.

The rookies lined up according to class number, with 68-19 being the first and 68-62 the last. All thirty-four rookies in each class stood in four lines. The instructors ordered them to extend their right arms to the next recruit's left shoulder and stay in a straight line, making the formation look uniform and professional.

Commanding officer Captain Gary Robbins of the Academy walked onto the stage in front of the recruits. "Good morning, Class. Today,

April 5, 1968, is a historic day in the New York City Police Department. We need all of you out their protection the streets of New York City. You'll be assigned to a veteran officer who will supervise you while on patrol. Listen to him and follow his orders. We can stop these riots soon, then we'll return to the Academy to continue your training.

"The buses outside will take you to 329 Broom Street to the Police Equipment Bureau, where you'll be issued uniforms all the other standard Police equipment, you'll need to stop these riots."

"We'll start by calling the names of your company sergeants. They are the liaison between the department and you. We choose company sergeants, because they have been in the military and have achieved the rank of master sergeant or higher."

He announced the names of the company sergeants. To Marvin's surprise, he was named as one of them. Everyone in the company 68-19 turned and looked at Marvin.

In shock, Marvin thought, *I'll have to do my Lee Marvin impression of the man in charge in the movie* The Dirty Dozen.

"All company sergeants, report to my office immediately," the commanding officer said, "Class, report to your assigned classroom. Class dismissed!"

Marvin met the other company sergeants, as they went down the steps to the commander's office. There was a U.S. retired military colonel, eleven retired majors, twenty-three lieutenants who just left the service, and

were master sergeants. All served in the Vietnam War. New York City civil services rules Allowed military time to be deducted from a recruit's age. The normal age limit was twenty-seven, but if a man were forty-seven and had twenty years in the military, he would deduct those twenty years from his age, and he would be Allowed to become a police officer.

They arrived at the commander's office and were immediately rushed in.

"Company sergeants, we don't have much time," Captain Robbins said. "I'll make this fast and to the point. The city's in deep shit. I want you to bring what you learned in the military to the police department. Those buses will take your class to the Police Equipment Bureau at 329

Broom Street, where your recruits will be issued their uniforms and police equipment. Then you'll return to your classrooms, where we'll wait and see if we need the recruits tonight. If the riots get out of hand, we will have no choice but to use all available manpower.

"We'll see what happens. We are playing this by ear. I know our plans will change as the situation warrants. Go to your classrooms and wait for the order to board the buses.

"Super Jew, please stay. I want to talk with you. There's something we have to do before you return to your classroom."

The company sergeants filed out, leaving just Captain Robbins and Marvin in the office.

"Super Jew, I just wanted to tell you that was some arrest you made yesterday. This is crazy day, but we must go downstairs for a press conference. It'll be a fast interview, and they'll take pictures. You'll be on TV news and in all the newspapers in the city and around the country. Just stay on message and don't wander into any other subject but the arrest. Look into the cameras and be serious. I'd don't want jokes and don't come off cocky. You'll be OK. I wish I had more time to give you the ins and outs of dealing with the press, but there's no time. Once that interview is over, we get out of here and on to the mean streets to keep the lid on this city. Got it? Any questions?"

"I just hope I'm not over my head." *I'll need to do my Walter Cronkite impression during the interview,* he thought.

As they took the elevator down to the pressroom, the captain looked extremely nervous.

"Look, captain, I'll do fine," Marvin said, trying to calm the commanding office down." Don't worry. This is a piece of cake."

"thanks, but we're all under a lot of pressure right now with what's going on in the city. Remember, there's civil unrest throughout most of the country. This could get out of hand fast. The last thing I want to do today is met the press.

They entered the pressroom and approached the podium. On the wall behind it was the logo of the New York City Police Department. Marvin and Captain Robbins stood on the small stage in front of the logo before a large group of reporters.

"Good morning," the captain said. "I'm sorry, but we have to make this press conference as fast as we can. We're needed out on the streets. Let me introduce you to Super Jew, who arrested the murderers yesterday. He was unarmed and had only one day on the job. He's a credit to the kind of people we're trying to bring into the greatest job in the world, working for the New York City Police Department."

TV cameras were rolling, and press cameras clicked rapidly.

"How'd you subdue all ten murderers?" one of the news reporters asked.

"I wish I could get into the details," Marvin replied, "but I was ordered by the district attorney's office not to discuss the details of the arrest, because there's a criminal case pending."

"Look, guys," Captain Robbins said. We must leave now to process the April 3rd class and prepare them to go out on the Streets tonight to stop the looting and rioting that's going on in our city.

As they reached the hall to the elevator, Captain Robbins told Marvin, "You handled yourself well back there. When we assign command, I'll give you any command or detail you want. I owe you. After you're off probation, I'll see if I can make you a third-grade detective. If you get into a jam on this job, I'll see if I can help you out of it. I promise.

"When you have someone helping you in the New York City Police Department, it's called having a rabbi to take care of you. It's ironic that you're Jewish, and you have a rabbi to care of you-on and off the job."

They laughed.

CHAPTER TWO

Let's Begin to Become a Cop

Marvin finally reached a typical high-school classroom, with rows of desks and a large blackboard at the front wall of the classroom. The instructor, Sergeant Roger Cummings, started the class by teaching the thirty-four recruits how to fill out police memo books. The memo was an official legal document that fit into an officer's back pocket, and the pages were numbered in sequence. Each memo book had its own ID number. The book began with the date and time, the officer's assignment, the time when he received the job, the deposition of the job, the time he went to the bathroom, what time he ate, and what time he resumed patrol. The most-important item was the time when the supervisor scratched, or signed, the memo book, which had to be done at least once each tour of duty to ensure the officer was on the job.

There was an art to filling out the memo book. Police officers were allotted twenty minutes twice each tour of duty for personal time, which was usually bathroom breaks. A veteran would start his twenty-minute personal on the ten minutes after hour. If nothing happened during that time, he wrote over the ten in his memo book to make it forty. Just like magic, he would kill a whole hour on his personal.

The memo book was a picture of what the officer did during his whole tour of duty. All memo books were stored during the officer's career in the New York City Police Department vault.

Marvin open the door and enter the classroom and walked to the back of the classroom and took the only empty seat in the room.

Sergeant Cummins stopped talking and looked at Marvin, "Did they tell you what's going on?"

"Not much. Its wait and see. If things get out of hand, they'll throw us out to quell the riots. Right now, they'll get us our uniforms and equipment in case we're needed. Looks like we'll be on the buses before lunch. At least, that was my impression."

The sergeant turned on an AM radio to 1010 WINS to listen for news about the riots. The whole class gathered around the radio to hear what was happening.

The reporter told them large demonstrations were in process in downtown Brooklyn on Fulton Street. Department stores were being looted and burned in broad daylight. Store owners are being beaten shot, trying to protect their stores. The reporter went on to report that there has been over 100-people shot and 36-people killed and over 500-arrest for violent crimes in the past 12-hours just in Brooklyn.

A store owner and his wife Mark and Patricia McCloskey armed themselves with guns to defend themselves and his property. The store owner's shot and killed seven looters and was hailed as a hero by the media and public.

"Hang onto your shorts," Jack Kegney, a recruit, said. "You'll be wearing them for a couple of days. We'll be on patrol today for sure. There's no way they'll let us go home at four o'clock.

The classroom door slammed open, and a captain and lieutenant rushed in wearing riot helmets and carrying night sticks. They bang the night stick on the floor several times of the classroom to gain the recruit's attention. "We need the recruits ready for patrol today. They're dying for help in the Twenty-first precinct.

Tom Manks, another recruit, walked to the captain and shouted out "Are you crazy?" Putting us on the street without training? We're unarmed, and I don't have a clue how to be a police officer." He tossed his shield at the captain and said, "I quit." He walks out of the door of the classroom.

The captain knew what they were thinking. "Everyone in class will be issued a service revolver and will be legally qualified to use and carry your gun today. After you are issued your uniforms, you'll return here and change into the uniforms, then you'll be taken by bus to the Police Firing Range in Rodman's Neck in the Bronx. You'll come back here for training in the use of deadly force and the use of necessary force to make arrests. That's the plan, but it might change as circumstances warrant."

I be a full-fledged police officer today, Marvin thought. The city must be desperate to put us on the street with no training.

On the Bus

Company Sergeant Marvin sat in the front of the bus, making sure Pete and Jim sat with him. A happy, festive mood filed the bus, with the men kidding around with each other. Marvin thought they were acting like school kids. If the bus driver was not complaining about all the noise and kidding around. It's worth it to let them have fun. He had to pretend and acted like Lee Marvin in the movie the *Dirty Dozen*, so he did not join in the festivities.

When they arrived at 349 Broom Street, all twenty-seven buses stopped in front. The door to Marvin's bus opened, and a police instructor boarded.

"Sergeant, take your company and line up in front of the building just like on the muster deck."

They stepped outside and lined up, like the recruits on the buses. A three-star deputy chief inspector with his aide, a captain, and a police officer with a portable radio, waited for them.

"That's a superior officer, Pete whispered to Marvin, standing in front of him. "He's an assistant chief inspector. There are only five of them in the whole department, and all oversee a borough. Only the police commissioner and chief inspector Stan Cohen are higher in rank. Maybe he's the one in charge of Manhattan."

All the police instructors stood in front of the assembled company and snapped to attention.

"Attention!" they shouted, making the recruits come to attention, too.

"Men, this is an emergency situation," the assistant chief inspector said. "We'll issue you your gray rookie uniforms with all your equipment, as well as your service revolver, but you must keep it the gun in the seal box and you will be issue ammo at the police firing range. If you take the gun out, you will be fired on the spot. You must qualify at the firing range before you can touch your service revolver.

"You'll be going up to the roof of the Equipment Bureau, where you'll be handed a large bag. You will then descend using the fire escape, stopping by each window on every floor to offer your bag. We'll fill your bag with police equipment. When you reach the ground floor, you'll be issued your service revolver in a sealed box. You must sign the uniform loan forms. The amount will be automatically deducted from your paycheck every two weeks. There's no interest. It's only five dollars per check.

"The service revolver is subsidized by the federal government, so your total cost is twelve dollars for the gun. The bullets are free. You'll be issued .38 caliber round-nose bullets at the firing range.

"The city is counting on you to keep the peace. God bless you and keep safe." He stared at them and looked at the formation of rookie cops and thought for a split second *about what's waiting for them when they go out on patrol to stop the riots in the city.* "Company 68-19, enter the building and take the stairs to the roof."

Marvin and his company were the first company to enter the building. They went to the roof, where they met a sergeant who gave them each a large bag.

"There are four windows on each floor Along the fire escape," he said. "Go to all four windows and hold out the bag, so the officer doesn't have to bend over to hand you your equipment," He helped them start their descent on the fire escape.

Marvin saw a long ladder with six steps that was attached the roof. And officer helped the recruits down the ladder. Marvin held onto the ladder, making sure it was secure, then he went down to the first window and saw a hand toss something into his bag. He moved to the next window. That continued until he reached the bottom of the fire escape.

At the last window, he was ordered to hand his full bag to the waiting officer and climb into the window on the ground floor to sign forms and be issued his Smith and Wesson six-inch, six-shot service revolver in a sealed box.

Marvin finally left the building and was ordered to board the bus and wait for

of his class. After the whole class was onboard, the captain came in and took roll call to make sure everyone was present. He ordered the driver to take them to Rodman's Neck firing range, where Marvin and the others would be taught to fire and legally carry their guns on and off-duty.

I never held a gun in my life, Marvin thought. *How the hell will they teach me to shoot a gun in ten minutes?*

As the bus went north to the Bronx, heading for City Island, the class saw the riots as they passed. On 125th Street and Third Avenue, Marvin saw a large crowd of over 100 looters, some carrying TV sets. Two looters in the middle of the crowd carried a large brand-new sofa still in its plastic cover with tags attached to the sofa in the middle of the street. A car drove down the street trailing a chain attached to a safe form a bank.

The rioters stopped the bus, throwing rocks and firing shots at the people inside the bus, all the recruits ducked for cover on the bus.

"Holly shit!" the bus driver said. "Hang on! "We're going right through them!"

The bus sped up and slammed into the crowd, running over some of the rioters. Six shots came in through the windows on the right side of the bus. Randy Cox, sitting beside a window three rows behind Marvin, was hit in the shoulder. Marvin ran to him. Other recruits came to assist Randy Cox, they all try to stop the bleeding.

Randy was in extreme pain, his shirt and dress suit covered in blood. Tom Barnes, another recruit, was an EMS before he became a cop. He removed his suit jacket and tried to stop the bleeding, but Randy went into shock and started to lose consciousness.

"We need to get him to a hospital quick!" Tom Barnes shouted.

The driver drove like he had a fire truck, going right through red lights, down the wrong side of the street, and speeding at eighty miles per hour to the emergency room of Harlem Hospital, where Marvin and six others carried Randy inside to the emergency room.

Staff members stopped what they were doing and rushed over. They took Randy into the emergency operation room and began working on him.

Marvin called police headquarters and informed them what happened. Within minutes, a police captain, four detectives, and two officers arrived to begin and investigation.

"This is a first in New York City Police Department history," the captain said. "Officer Randy Cox will be retired with three-fourths disability pension within two days on the job."

"What's three-fourths disability?" Marvin asked.

"When an officer is permanently injured on the job, and can't perform police work anymore, he is eligible for a pension for

of his life, no matter how long he's been on the job. Let this be a lesson to you. Always report injuries that happen on the job. You never know when one will be permanent.

The doctor came out and spoke to the captain. "The officer on his way to the operating room. We must remove a bullet lodged in his chest. He's got a fifty-fifty odd of survival. We'll do whatever we can to save him. I give you my word."

"Thank, Doc."

The doctor turned and went into the operation room.

"We'll notify his family," the captain told one of the detectives. He turned to Marvin. "Give the detective your name, shield number, and Police Academy company number. You look familiar were you on the news? Are you the recruit named Marvin Levey who made those ten homicide arrest yesterday?

"Yes, Sir."

"Super Jew, you're having a whole career in two days on the job." The captain used his radio to call headquarters. "Tell the dispatcher to have a police escort for this bus, to the shooting range."

Five minutes later, two highway patrol cars arrived at Harlem hospital to escort Marvin's bus to the shooting range.

"You men will continue to the shooting rage," the captain told them. "We need you guys tonight, and I mean it."

Company 68-19 boarded the bus the constant sound of police sirens announcing their escort.

The mood in the bus turned serious. Some of the recruits wanted the bus to turn around and go back to the rioters in 125th Street and make some arrests. Others wanted to stay with Randy until his family arrived at the hospital.

As the bus rerouted to the range, they passed burning cars and stores. When they passed groups of rioters, all three vehicles were pelted with rocks. Some smashed the bus windows.

Finally, the bus was trapped by burned out cars in the middle of the street and was quickly surrounded by angry rioters. The driver had nowhere to go. Rioters boarded the bus with baseball bats, and Marvin heard gunfire in the background.

What have I gotten myself into? He wondered. *This is crazy! You can get seriously hurt doing police work.*

Looking out the window, he saw the highway cops were down laying on the street, being stomped and kicked. The rioters were grabbing for the officer's guns that were still in their holsters. He and Pete immediately began shouting.

"Let's go help those highway cops! Everybody off the bus! It's showtime!"

Marvin and Pete led the charge. They grabbed a tall black man in his late fifties who look like a drug addict, wrestled him down, and found a loaded gun. Marvin took the gun away from him and fired into the crowd. Within moments, the crowd dispersed. Three rioters lay dead on the street laying on the street next to the four semi-conscious injured highway cops.

Marvin and Pete ran to the downed officers, their uniforms tattered and guns missing. The rookie Tom Barnes the former EMS recruit rendered aid, while another man used the radio in the highway cops police to call for an ambulance and assistance.

Marvin looked around and couldn't believe that some in his recruits in his company made arrests, especially since none of them had handcuffs. They put five prisoners in the back of the bus.

While waiting for help to arrive, four recruits started kicking the shit out of the prisoners. More recruits joined them. Marvin, Pete, and Jim saw the scene, Marin said, "Look, Guys, I know how we feel, but we have to stop this shit with the prisoners."

A recruit named Hennessey said, "Just let me have one more kick in the head for this son of a bitch who beat up those highway cops. I want him to know what they felt. Then I'll stop if you just give me one more kick to this skel's head, Super Jew."

"OK. Just one more kick."

Hennessey gave the man a roundhouse kick that opened the prisoner's head and Almost took it off his spine. The man felt unconscious and had shallow breathing for a few seconds, then he went limp.

Tom Barnes examined him and said, "this one's dead."

The whole bus fell silent. The remaining prisoners began crying and begging not to be hurt anymore.

"We're in deep shit if this gets out," Marvin said. "We have to cover our asses. We'll tell the detectives the rioters were robbing this idiot, and they killed him. We can blame it all on the rioters. What do you think? Does anyone have a better story?"

"I think that's our other choice and it's a story that I hope will work," one man said. "It's not about saving our jobs. It's about staying out of jail. We have to all tell the same story and stick to it."

The other agreed.

"What about my running over those rioters?" the driver asked.

"It never happened," Marvin said.

The recruits nodded.

"We have to let the four prisoners escape, Marvin said. "if they come back, we'll arrest them and try them for killing the prisoner laying on the floor of the bus.

"You'll never hear form us again!" one prisoner said. All the prisoners agreed."

Marvin took their ID's "If we hear you want to give us any trouble, we'll take care of you four. Got that?'

The four rans from the bus, limping away as fast as they could.

Marvin waited for the investigator and ambulance to arrive, but it seemed to take forever. Through the front window, he saw an angry crowd forming outside, Marvin finally decide to leave the scene with the four injured highway patrolmen and one dead rioter and head for the range.

The driver pulled away. They made it to Rodman's Neck without further incident.

CHAPTER THREE

Rodman's Neck Firing Range

The bus pulled up to the gate at the firing range, and officer boarded and looked around. "They're been looking for the bus from Harlem. What happened to you guys? There were three dead bodies at your last location and two burned-out police cars. The four highway cops are missing."

"It's a long story," Marvin said. "there's no police radio in this bus, so we had to wing it. We have four serious injured highway police officers with us and one dead victim of a robbery on the bus. What should we do now?"

"Wait here until I call for help." The range officer ran to his booth and called headquarters. Within minutes, the bus was surrounded by police cars and ambulances.

A police captain boarded the bus and took one long look around the bus before he asked, "What happened?"

The policemen and EMS rush over to the four injured officers and carried them to a waiting ambulance.

Marvin told the captain and investigators their story in front of the whole bus without blinking.

"Supe Jew, I know you guys don't know shit about police work, but you have to stay at a crime scene and wait for detectives to conduct an investigation," the captain said. "Who shot the three people and killed them?"

"I did."

"How?"

Marvin told them that he and his partner grabbed one of the armed rioters when they got off the bus and wrestled him to the ground.

"I was lucky and got his gun away from him before the rioter could have shot me or the other rookie's. I fired and emptied the gun into the crowd. I must've hit at least three other rioters in the crowd."

"Holly shit!" Marvin, you really are a Super Jew. Listen to me carefully. Your answer is particularly important. You can only use deadly force when your life or the life of someone else life is in immediate danger. You can't use deadly force for stealing property, unless you feel your life is threatened. That the law."

"All you recruit must remember that. Never, never tell an investigator you shot someone for stealing property. You will go to jail for it. Now, Marvin, tell me why you shot those three people."

Marvin is unsure what to say. He took a deep breath, lowered his voice, and answered the captain question. "Because I felt that my life and my fellow recruit's life were in danger."

"You just passed your first test. The shooting was justified. Where's the gun?"

"In my pocket, Captain."

"Let me have it. You aren't Allowed to carry a gun until you're been qualified at the range."

Marvin handed him the gun. The captain examined it and popped open the clip.

"That's a Glock 9mm with a fifteen-shot clip. It's empty. You might have shot sixteen rounds into the crowd. Have the detectives go to the scene and local hospitals to see if he hit anyone else. Before I forget, make sure the victim's families are notified. If they can't afford a funeral, the city will cover it. The poor bastard was in the wrong place at the wrong time."

"Captain, you're so right."

All the recruits and the bus diver laughed.

"Captain," the detective said, "we have to wait before we can go to Harlem. It's not safe there yet."

"What the hell is this city coming to?" the captain asked. "OK. This case is closed. On the report, the finding will be that the condition was corrected by Police Academy Class 68-19 will from now on will be called the A Team and will be the first company sent into quell riots. When this situation is over, the A Team will have their choice of assignments. Even though I just said assignments, the police jargon is details. That includes mounted unit or highway patrol. There are many other details, too many to mention at this time, that any cop would love to have.

"It would be a waste of time to qualify you guys to carry your guns, since you already shot and killed three bad guys on the way over here. Marvin, I mean Super Jew, you and your company will get a meritorious police medal for what you did today. As for you, Super Jew, I will recommend you for third-grade detective after you graduate form the Academy."

"Thank you, Sir. I don't know what to say."

The company gave the captain and their superior officers a standing ovation.

CHAPTER FOUR

At the Police Firing Range

Company 68-19, now called the A Team, entered the classroom at the range. A profoundly serious, tough, stern range officer waited for them to take their seats.

"My name is Range Officer Pete Emelanchick. I was a professional football player for the Philadelphia Eagles and the backup for Mike Ditka. This is my twenty-fifth year on the job, and I can retire anytime I want to. I have my time in. But I love this job and most of you will feel the same way I do."

"Thank God, the department has the backing of the public and politicians to do our job to stop the rioting. Could you image if the public and politicians turned their back on us? We could never stop the riots or protect the good citizen of the city? I would retire in a heartbeat and get the hell out of the city as fast as I can!"

Pete Cahill shouted out, "That would never happen, where politicians would come after cops in the middle of a crisis! That would be the most idiotic thing any normal person would do."

The range officer and the whole class agreed with Pete Cahill.

The range officer looks at the class, "We'll be going over the laws concerning the use of deadly physical force and necessary force to legally effect an arrest.

"First, the use of necessary force to effect a person who is resisting arrest. You can use all the necessary force that you deem necessary to protect yourself and other police officers to prevent from being injured or killed while subduing a prisoner. Unless you're been a cop all alone with a suspect in the middle of the night in a fight for your life and you're being punched, kicked, bitten, and you're total exhausted trying from being killed or injured with your own gun....you're opinion on the use of necessary force of police officer will definitely change, your opinion about a using a choke hold and putting a knee on some low life's back will definitely be accepted in subduing a prisoner.

"Making resisting arrest is like working in a meat packing plant making sausage. When a person is resisting and being arrested, it looks ugly and messy when the officer is fighting for his or her life trying to restrain the prisoner. Remember you are carrying a loaded gun that can be taken away from you during the fight, don't laugh. Statistics show that most cops are shot by their own guns by perps that resist arrest and get the upper hand in a wrestling match on the ground with the police officer.

"Couple of examples, we had a 13-year old girl who just committed a felonious assault on her principal in her school. She stabbed him with a scissors in his head. The principal latter died from the stabbing. The student did not want to be arrested. She resisted arrest. She grabs the arresting officer's gun while she was wrestling on the floor with the cops. It took six cops to restrain her and take the gun back from her and handcuff her." A lesson to be learned is if a person doesn't want to be arrested. It's almost impossible to place the prisoner in handcuffs. Without placing the prisoner in a headlock and putting your knee on the prisoner's back.

"Let me give you another example, a car stopped for speeding and passing a red light. Maybe the reason the driver is speeding and passing red lights is he just committed a crime and he is trying flee the scene of a crime?"

"When you have physical contact with the public you don't know if the person you are taking to is wanted for a crime or maybe he or she just committed a crime. They are thinking that you know their criminal situation, and you are going to arrest them. You do not know what is in the mind of the person you stopped. Your gun can be up for grabs and can be used against you and your partner. Interaction with the public is serious shit. Take all interactions with the public with extreme caution."

"I'll give you a real incident that I had five years ago when I work in the 75th precincts. Me and my partner Don, patrolling in a police car, stop at a red traffic light when we both saw an old broken-down beat-up Chevy two blocks away speeding through a red light. We estimate the driver was going at least 80-miles an hour. My partner puts the lights and siren on, and I pull the police car out into the intersection to block the speeding car. The Chevy came to a screeching halt in front of our police car. We both jump out of the police car and approach the Chevy. We separate one on each side of the car, with our guns out pointed to the ground.

The driver has his daughter, about fifteen-years old in the passenger side of the car with her seat belt on. She has a blank expression on her face doesn't say a word during the whole time of the traffic stop.

I ask the driver for his driver license and auto registration. The driver cooperates, and hands me the paperwork. He automatically puts both hands on the steering wheel, so I clearly see his hands. He turns the car ignition off; my partner and I feel very safe. I looked at his license and his name and registration and all was in order. I said, "Do you know why we stop you, Mr. Winter?"

Mr. Winter, "Yes, I ran a red light. I was in a rush taking my daughter to the airport, she must make her flight to Prague, Czechoslovakia to be with her sick grandmother who is dying of cancer. If she misses this flight, the next one isn't until next week and that might be too late to see her dying grandmother. I just picked her up at my ex-wife's house Jane, to take her to the airport."

I ask Mr. Winter is if he has any proof of the flight. He produces a piece of paper with the TWA fight number, the time of the flight, the gate number and the destination Prague, Czechoslovakia scheduled from LaGuardia airport. The flight was less than an hour and a half from the time of the car stop. I turn to my partner who signals to me to give him one traffic ticket for going through the red light and let him go.

I told Mr. Winter we are going to rush writing the traffic ticket, then you could leave for the airport. If you go to traffic court, we could explain to the traffic court judge of the circumstances. I would vouch for you in court and I believe the case will be dismissed.

He said, "Thank you."

I gave him the ticket at 8:15 PM. I said just as a passing thought, Mr. Winter "Isn't Prague behind the iron curtain and our country has no relation with them." Mr. Winter answered "Yes, and once you're in Prague it's Almost impossible for the United States to bring you back to the states unless you want to come back. My daughter promises me she'll be coming back."

"The next morning on the news the big story is Jane Winter's murder! There was a kidnapped note left behind asking for money. The detectives would think the daughter is missing and might be a kidnapped victim.

Jane Winter is murdered and her home is burglarized ten-minutes and just blocks from where we made the car stop. when we issued Mr. Winter the traffic ticket.

I figured it out that Mr. Winter made it look like someone else killed his wife in the house. To give them time to escape to Prague, Czechoslovakia. That's why he and his daughter ransacked the house and left the ransom note.

When I heard the news on the radio, I immediately realized that we stopped the possible murderer, Mr. Winter, right after his wife was discovered murdered.

I stopped what I was doing and called the detectives at the major case squad. I spoke to Detective Bob Cromwell.

Detective Cromwell, "May I help you."

"I am police officer Pete Emelanchick; I think I have information on the Winter's murder. I believe I pulled over the husband of Jane Winter and her daughter was in the car. I gave him a summon number for going through a red light at 8:15 PM. They were going to LaGuardia airport to board a TWA fight to Prague, Czechoslovakia. He said to visit their sick grandmother."

Detective Cromwell "WOW! Pete it's OK for me to call you Pete?"

"Sure."

"We were trying to contact the husband to get some info. Pete, the info you just gave us could solve the murder case. You put the husband and daughter just four blocks from the scene of the wife murder just ten minutes from the time of crime. We will get a copy of the traffic summons and take a good look at it. I'll get in touch with your command and with the info you gave us you should get a commendation or promotion."

"We will check it out the info you gave us. I'll get back to you in about a week. Pete, what's your command, shield number and tax registration number?"

"It's the 75th precinct in Brooklyn," then Pete gave the detective all the other info he requested."

"Thanks," they both hung up the phone.

Two weeks later Detective Bob Cromwell met Pete Emelanchick in the captain's officer and gave them all the details of the Jane Winter's murder case.

Detective Cromwell said, "The suspects fled to Czechoslovakia and both the Winters have asked for political asylum. The husband and daughter have been interviewed by the police in Prague."

"The U.S. Marshals' sent us all the information from interview. The two police officers, Pete Emelanchick and his partner are incredibly lucky guys. They should buy a lotto ticket today. What the suspects confessed to the Prague police and said, "They both shot and killed Jane Winter with their guns. She was a bitch and made both their life's miserable. When you stopped them, their guns were under the car seats fully loaded. They did not know if you knew that they just committed murder. If you or your partner asked about where or what happened at Jane Winter house or gave the impression that you knew about the murder, they both would have shot you and your partner. This is from the statement they gave to the U.S. Marshal's."

Detective Cromwell went into more detail about the investigation, finished and ended the meeting by saying, "The case is in proper international channels to extradite the Winter's back to New York City to be tried in Criminal court for murder. Pete you and your partner solved the murder case. And this goes to show you that a simple traffic summon is the key piece of evidence in a police investigation to solve the case."

Range officer Pete Emelanchick points to his commendation medal on his uniform with a big smile on his face.

There is another murder case that was solve by a parking summon. The Son of Sam case in Brooklyn. The police officer gave a car a parking summons for blocking a fire hydrant. About a half-hour latter there is a murder of a young couple in the park where the car that got the summon is parked. The detectives of the 62nd precinct check-out all the parking tickets that were issue on the day of the murders near the scene of the crime. They found the owner of the car that got the summon, David Berkowitz who lived in the Bronx. They went to the Berkowitz's house and one look at him you know he fit the description of the murder. After interviewing him. The detectives recovered the 44-caliber gun that was used in 6-murders and wounding of 7 other victims. There another example of a parking ticket used to solve major case. Summons are important to solving crimes."

Range officer Pete Emelanchick looks at the class, "The point I'm trying to make is you just never know what's in the mind of the citizen that you encounter or if the last parking ticket you just issue will be used to solve a major crime. Always be alert and always call the detectives with information. You never know if the info will solve the case. Any questions?"

"Yes", One of the recruits asks, "Can we use a headlock or choke hold on a person resisting arrest to subdue the prisoner?"

The range officer answered. "Yes, that is the law and you are protected by the New York State penal law. All the courts have sided with the police officers that the use of a choke holds is legal, in fact, by having the prisoner semiconscious you are saving the prisoner's life by not having to shoot him. Most prisoners don't die from a headlock or by being choked and most cops prevent being injured by using headlock and choke holds."

"Look guys If I can teach you just one important lesson that all Hair bags (Hair bags are cops that have a lot of time on the job.) learn on the job is your most important assignment as a police officer is to go home to your family safe and sound in the same condition that you came to work, uninjured. This is the motto of the New York Police Department. *I would rather be judge by 12 people on a jury. Than to be carried by six Pallbearers carrying your coffin.*"

You are covered like a rug when you use physical force to effect an arrest. What do you think the politicians are going to do, defund the New York City Police department for a couple of bad interactions with criminals? That will never happen in my lifetime!"

What are the victims of vicious crimes going to do, who will they call when they need a cop? Ghost busters?"

The whole classroom erupted in laughter.

We have to get on to the most important subject using deadly physical force."

"There are two categories of police officers when it comes to using deadly physical force. The first category of police officer will shoot the instant he or she see a gun in a person's hand."

"The second category of police officer will wait till the criminal fires his gun at the police officer before he or she shoots back. Recruits there a lot to say about both categories. If you shoot the instant, you see a gun you might be making the biggest mistake of your life. Not all situations seem to be what they appear to be. For instance, I was called for a robbery in progress. We came upon the scene where a man is holding a gun and sitting on top of another man cover with blood. Me and my partner took out our guns and pointed the guns at the man with the gun and shouted out for the man to drop the gun! We did not shoot. We waited to see if the man with the gun pointed the gun at us. We both would have shot him. The man with the gun drops the gun and just sat there. One of the people in crowd rush over to us and told us that the man with the gun does not understand English and only speaks Russian. And the man with the gun is the victim of the robbery and he wrestled the gun away from the robber who he subdues. If we used Category one, we would have killed the wrong man. Recruits you have to pick which category you fit into."

"The use of deadly physical force is allowed only when your life or someone else's life is in immediate danger. You can't use deadly physical force for stealing property."

"That's Almost the exact words the captain said when we took down the three asses who tried to storm us on the bus and kill us," Marvin said.

"OK, A Team lined up at the firing range. Waiting for each man was a Smith and Wesson service revolver and eight shots is an open box, along with a headset and shooting goggles. The target was six feet in front of them.

"OK, A Team," the range officer said over the loudspeaker. "Put on your goggles and headset. You each will fire eight shots. Pick up your service revolver. Never point it at anyone. Always point the gun downrange."

"On the side of the gun is a small slide. With your thumb, slide that forward, and the cylinder will pop open. Load six rounds into the chamber and point the gun at the target."

He paused. "Firing line ready? Ready on the right? Ready on the left? Now fire!"

Marvin fired all six rounds but missed the target. He wasn't the only recruit in his class that miss the target. Pete, the range officer, came over to score him. He looked at the target and then put eight holes in it with his pen.

"Super Jew, you passed." The range officer announced.

"What do I do with the extra two bullets?"

"Keep them. You might need those rounds in an emergency."

"Thanks. Are we done? What's next?"

"OK, A Team, "the range officer said. "You all passed. You'll qualified to carry your firearms on and off duty. Leave the revolver on the ground in front of you for the next police company to use. Go back to the bus and get onboard for your trip back to the Academy. May God be with all of you."

Four police cruisers waited to escort the bus back to the academy. The bus driver followed the police cruisers who turned on the lights and siren, as they departed. They took the east side of Manhattan route on the FDR drive, which was a lot safer.

CHAPTER FIVE

In One Door and Out In the Streets of Brooklyn

It was eight o'clock in the evening and already dark when the A Team arrived back at the Academy. As Marvin exited the bus, he saw and smelled smoke coming from the east. The recruits still wore their suits and ties, as they headed toward their classroom.

They had Already been on the job for twelve hours, but Marvin felt a rush of excitement, almost like when he played football at Lincoln High school. He was not tired, and he wanted to help stop the riots.

They raced up the stairs to change into their recruit uniforms and try on their new Sam Browne belts that held their handcuffs, gun, holsters, extra bullets, flashlights, and pens. Marvin took his service revolver from the sealed box and tried to load it, but he had trouble. He put all six bullets into the cylinder, but he held it with the barrel pointing up, so the bullets fell out on to the floor.

Pete Cahill came over. "Super Jew hold it with the barrel of the gun pointing down to the floor. Use your left hand and hold the gun in your palm of your hand with two middle fingers wrapped around the open cylinder. The other fingers hold the gun. That always works when you reload."

"Thanks, Pete." Marvin tried it with success.

No one in the class knew where the police accessories belonged on their police belts. Pete opened a book that showed a picture of a police officer wearing all his accessories in the proper places. The company members copied that carefully. One of the recruits is left-handed was totally confused about how to use his belt, but Pete helped him figure it out.

The Academy instructor entered the room. "New York Governor Nelson Rockefeller signed an order placing New York City in a state of emergency, and he called in the National Guard. They won't be in place until tomorrow, so you recruit is the thin blue line keeping the peace in the city. You'll go to the Twenty-first Precinct in Brooklyn, where riots and looting are in progress. Until you're ready to go on patrol, I'll give you a lesson on how to fill out your memo books."

He walked to the blackboard and wrote *Memo* on the board, but before he could write *Book* the classroom door banged open, and a captain in full riot gear rushed into the front of the classroom.

"No time for any classroom work," the captain announced. "They're dying for help in the Twenty-first Precinct. Let's get to the bus, now!"

In their brand-new gray recruit uniforms and no training, the A Team left the Academy and boarded the bus again. They traveled without any interior lights. As they passed over the Manhattan Bridge, the men smelled smoke and heard gunfire from the other side. Marvin and the other ducked behind their seats, as the approached the Brooklyn side of the bridge. Marvin drew his gun and held it in his right hand.

The bus, with no lights on, sneaked around the corner at Adam Street and parked behind Brooklyn Borough Hall on Fulton Street and Adam Street. A large crowd of rioters were breaking into Gimbels Department Store and E.J. Korvette's Department Store on Fulton Street only two blocks away stealing anything that was not nailed down from the stores.

The captain, followed by his driver, came onto the bus. "Men, this is martial law. Do whatever you have to do to clear the streets in front of the department stores and hold the territory until we are relieved."

"One question, Sir," Marvin asked. "Can we shoot the looters?"

"Yes. Governor Rockefeller has declared martial law in the city. The department will back you if you have to shoot the rioters."

The captain drew his gun. "Recruits, follow me!"

They walked down the street and approached the crowd. The captain fired once into the air, and the crowd ran from E.J.Korvettes, but some of the looters turned toward the approaching police force. The captain shot and hit two of the looters, dropping them instantly.

Marvin saw the captain fire his gun and aimed at the looters who refused to run away. He fired all six rounds into the crowd, hitting four more looters. Most of the company opened fire. A moment later, dozens of wounded looters lay on the ground.

ran away.

Fulton Street was cleared of rioters and looters in minutes. The captain using his radio to call for ambulances, ordered all the wounded looters under arrest, then he assigned recruits to arrest them. The captain Then he ordered that if a looter look dead just leave him in the Street for the detectives to investigate."

The remaining recruits stood in front of the department store with orders to shoot or arrest any looters.

"Men, you did a great job tonight," the captain told everyone. "We'll use the bus as a detention and processing center for any prisoners. You'll work in pairs. When things quiet down, you don't need both of you out together. We call that breaking it up. The job doesn't expect recruits to stand on the streets for twelve hours at a time.

"OK, A Team. Pick your partners. If you don't have one, I'll assign one. It looks like we'll be here until eight in the morning, hopefully that's when our relief will arrive. When you break it up, try to take a nap in the Paramount Theater on Flatbush Avenue. If you get hungry, you can get a bite to eat at Junior's Café on Flatbush Avenue. It's on the arm for us. Men, take your posts."

Marvin partnered with Pete Cahill, Marvin took the first shift, which would last two hours.

"I'll be sleeping in the Paramount Theater if you need me," Pete said.

"Got it. If there's trouble, I'll come get you."

Fulton Street from Flatbush Avenue to Adams Street was a remarkably busy business district with many large department stores and mom-pop stores. After the looters fled, it seemed like the safest place on earth for all the cops on duty.

Marvin used a pay telephone to call his mother and tell her where he was and that he was all right.

"You have to get home!" Edith demanded. "I need you. I'm worried sick about you. There is a curfew in the city. I can't leave the house, and there are riots, looting, and muggings everywhere. Who'll protect me while you're gone?"

"Mom, I'll get home as soon as I can, but it won't be until morning. If anything happens, call 911 and tell them you're a family member of the service. Stay home and be safe. I must go, now. Love you."

I'm losing all control over you, Marvin. You sure have changed. I'll pray for you and all the other members of the police department to be safe."

Marvin returned to his post in front of E.J.Korvette's, where he saw a police officer in a blue uniform walking his footpost.

"Let's ask him about what we have to do," Marvin said.

They stopped the officer, assuming he had time to talk to them and would understand police procedure.

"I have to ask you," Marvin said, "what's is this police work all about? This is our first day on the job. And we have had no training on what to do."

"How the hell would I know? He replied. "I'm in the February 1968 police Academy class."

The rookies laughed.

"All right," Marvin told the others around him. "We just have to use common sense and we'll be fine."

A police sergeant ran up to the recruits with a police radio that had very loud panicked voices shouting 10-13, 10-13 coming from radio. "I need ten officers to come with me right now. There's a running 10-13 on the train."

"What's a 10-13?" Marvin asked.

He stared at them. "You don't know what a 10-13 is? It means a fellow cop's in trouble. When a 10-13 comes over the radio, all cops stop what they're doing and respond as fast as possible to render aid and assistant to the cops that need help. Nothing is more important than helping a fellow cop. We've got a cop on the train who's been shot by rioters with his own gun. We have to save him and hopefully arrest the people who did this to the cop!"

Marvin and nine others left the front of the department store and ran down to Court Street Station, where they met twenty more cops. The train doors were closed, and screams came from inside the car. The captain walked up to the conductor who was able to control the train doors.

"Open just one door and let us in," the captain said. "Don't open any other doors."

"OK," the train conductor said.

The captain turned to Marvin and the others. "I want arrests, but if any of those bastrads give you a hard time, you can kick the living shit out of them. Got it?"

"Yes, Sir!" they shouted.

Entering the train, they saw the transit cop on the floor. Thirteen rioters tried to leave the train.

Marvin had his nightstick in hand, ready to use. The captain and his driver swung their nightsticks. One rioter was hit on the head and went down, clutching his head that is cover with blood.

"Arrest him!" the captain told a recruit.

The captain went to the transit cop, who lay in a pool of his own blood. His service revolver was missing. The captain and an EMT started working on the cop, trying to keep him Alive.

"Which one of you idiots has this man's gun?" the captain demanded.

None of the rioters moved. A recruit found the gun under one of the seats.

The captain turned to the rioters. "Which one of you shot him? I want an answer right now!"

No one spoke.

"Men," he told the thirty cops standing behind him. "Get me an answer!"

That started another riot. Marvin and the officers began kicking the shit out the rioters. They soon found the man who shot the cop. The rioters who could still move pointed at this one guy.

"Arrest all of them except the one who shot the cop," the captain said. "Will take special care of him."

Marvin made his second arrest in two days, using his brand-new handcuffs on the prisoner's hands in front of his body.

"Officer never handcuff a prisoner in the front," the captain said. "Always do it from the back. If you handcuff him from the front, he can use both hands to chock you from behind with the cuffs. Worse, he might grab your gun."

He looked at Marvin, "Didn't they teach you anything at the Academy?"

"No, Sir. This is our first night on patrol. We never had any training at the Academy."

"OK, Officer, the captain said in a softer voice "You'll have the best training any officer can get. You'll learn your job on the street."

He turned to the group of officers. "I want to show you recruits what happens to a perp who assaults or injures a member of the police force. After we clear everyone else out, I want you recruits to stay and watch.

"Tell the conductor to close the door. We have some business to take care of."

The captain and the two large cops began kicking the shit out of the man who shot the transit cop. After the beating, they dragged him to a waiting ambulance while his hands are cuffed behind him. The captain covered the man with a trench coat and floppy hat.

"Why are you putting a coat and hat on the prisoner?"

"In case there are TV reporters at the hospital. It doesn't look good when a prisoner's all beat up. That's a lesson to be learned in all police commands. We've got a large floppy and an old detective's trench coat just for cop fighters. The cop fighters know all about it. Word about the beating gets around on the street, and it makes it a lot easier for the next cop who must deal with the skels. Super Jew never bring in a prisoner to the station house who has been charged with resisting arrest without blood coming from the prisoner. Got that?"

Marvin nodded and left the train to process the prisoner. He found a police van waiting for the two of them.

Marvin helped the prisoner up the three steps into the bus. The sergeant ordered Marvin and the prisoner to stand in front of the bus, so he could take a Polaroid photograph. He pulled out the film and waved it to help the picture dry, then he blew on it.

He looked at the photo and asked, "Officer, what your name?"

"Marvin Levey."

"Are you the one they call Super Jew?"

"Yes, this is my eleventh arrest in two days."

"You're going to break he department record for the number of arrests. Look at this picture. Your smiling. It looks like you two are on vacation. If this goes to trial, they the jury will take one look at this picture won't take the arrest seriously. Let's do another one."

Marvin made sure he looked serious the next time. He spent the next two hours filling out arrest forms on the bus.

The sergeant gave him fifteen large index cards in different colors-blue, white, yellow, and red. Each color card would go to a different law enforcement agency, with the red one going to the FBI. He filled out the personal information on the cards, then he escorted the prisoner onto the bus to have him fingerprinted. The detective didn't have a gun, since the prisoner would be behind him for the fingerprinting.

"Did the prisoner give you a hard time?" the detective asked. "If he did, you have to take him off the bus and tune him up."

"No. He behaved."

"Officer, remove the prisoner's handcuffs."

The detective gave the man a rag with Alcohol on it, and he wiped his fingers with it. The detective fingerprinted the man, to a look at the prints and then he nodded his head up and down of approval.

"OK, these prints will pass."

"What are you looking for?" Marvin asked.

"See the swirls? Here is the delta on the thumb. You put ten fingers together, and the odds of anyone else having the same fingerprints are in the billions."

"Give all the prisoner's arrest paperwork to the sergeant, and he'll give it to a police courier to take to BCI. You have to wait for the prisoner's rap sheet before you can go to court."

"I have a couple questions. What's BCI? How long will I have to wait for the rap sheet? What's a rap sheet?"

"Are you the cop they call Super Jew?"

"Yes."

"OK. I'll go through the procedures for making an arrest. BCI is where the prisoner's fingerprints go. They have a direct link to all the arrest records in the free world, and the FBI data base. The prints will show if the prisoner is wanted or if the prints match any crimes under investigation. That help the judge determine if the prisoner is eligible for bail.

"Here's the good news. It takes about twelve hours to get the rap sheet back, and you're on overtime while you wait. In the police department, we call that collars for dollars. You can make a nice living making lots of collars.

"After you give the sergeant the paperwork and you log in the prisoner in the cell, the police car will take you the courthouse. Sign into the police room and go to sleep until they call you to appear in the courtroom for the prisoner's arrangement."

CHAPTER SIX

Welcome to New York City Criminal Court

Marvin arrived at the New York City Criminal Court at 120 Schermerhorn Street, Brooklyn, New York, 11201. Brooklyn Central Court Building was built in 1932. The architects were Collins and Collins, who created the building in the style of Renaissance Revival/Beaux Arts classical. The cost of construction at the time was astonishing $440,000. Dollars of taxpayer's money. Marvin thought *maybe someone should investigate where all that money went to build the courthouse.*

Marvin entered the courthouse and looked around, concluding the place was a dump. It looked completely run down.

He helped his prisoner up the stairs and rang the bell at a solid metal door. A police officer looked out the peephole and then opened the door to allow Marvin and his prisoner into Central booking, the last step before arraigning the prisoner before the judge.

"Let me have your paperwork," the officer said, looking it over. "Officer Levey, you have a long wait before you'll be called to the courtroom. It's been a very busy day."

He searched the prisoner. "Log the prisoner into the cell, then go up to see the assistant district attorney at the office and fill out your sworn arrest affidavit. After that you can go to the police room and wait to be called to the courtroom for the arraignment."

"Where's the district attorney's room?"

"One flight up."

Marvin went to the DAs' room and saw it was full of police officers waiting to be called to fill out their arrest affidavits. He logged in and asked the clerk how long his wait would be.

"About eight hours," the clerk said. "The clerk said. "The assistant DA has to interview you about the arrest before the DA will fill out the affidavit. If you want, you can get lost for six hours, then come back and wait for your turn."

CHAPTER SEVEN

The Jury Box Bar

Marvin met another cop in the hall, and they hit it off.

"My name's Phil Barnes," he said. I've got two years on the job. I thought I'd seen everything, but these last two days are the icing on the cake. I've been on at least twenty 10-13's in last two days. The arrest I made is for shooting a cop with his own gun. Thank God the cop will be OK."

"I know, Marvin said. "I was there when the highway cops were shot in Harlem."

"Harlem? This cop was shot in Williamsburg, Brooklyn."

Marvin was surprised. "You mean there are more cops who were shot?"

"Not only shot. Some were beaten and severely injured."

"Let's get out of here. We've got six hours to kill."

"There's a bar on Livingston Street called the Jury Box. A lot of cops hang out there until they are called to court. They've TV's and a telephone that the bridgeman in court uses to notify you what time to appear for the arraignment."

Marvin's multiple arrest on the subway train came up. Phil had already heard the story and immediately started calling Marvin Super Jew.

The Jury Box bar was full of cops, lawyers, and court personnel waiting to be called into court. There were also women who love being with policemen that hung out at the bar.

The bartender had been a famous cop. He was in the newspapers and on TV for shooting it out with the Black Liberation Army in front of police headquarters on New Year's Eve. His part-time job was to work as a bartender.

The problem was police officers were banned from working in any store that sold alcohol. It was an open secret in the department that some officers worked in bars, but no one cared.

"Super Jew give the bartender your name and shield number, "Phil said, "so when the bridge officer calls, he'll tell you when to report to court. The most-important thing right now is to order a good stiff drink."

Marvin gave the bartender his name and shield number.

"Are you Super Jew?"

"Yes."

The bartender turned toward the crowded room. "We got hero here at the bar, Super Jew!"

The patrons gave Marvin a standing ovation.

"What'll you guys have to drink?" The bartender asked. "It's on the arm."

"Seven and seven."

"I'll have the same," Marvin said, then he turned to Phil. "What's a seven and seven?"

"It's Seagram's Seven with 7-Up on the rocks."

Two beautiful women came up to them, in their late twenties, one woman was tall at over five-feet-nine-inches, wearing white boots with heels, bell-bottomed black pants with wide black belts, and tight while silk blouses. The other women were wearing a business suit with high heel shoes. The shorter women have beautiful long, blonde hair, gorgeous faces with dimples, perfect white teeth, and perfect bodies. They both looked like two twin fashion models.

Marvin looked at both women and immediately was attracted to both women. As both women approached, Marvin suddenly felt shy and nervous.

Before Marvin could speak, the bartender came back. "Big Mo Dash wants to meet Super Jew."

"Who's Mo Dash?" Marvin asked.

"You've got to be kidding," the bartender said. "You don't know Big Mo? He runs this city; this bar is his office. A lot of politicians, judges, lawyers, and movers and shakers come in to make important deals with him. You should be honored to meet him. He can do a lot for your police career."

Phil and the two women were shocked at the news.

"Super Jew don't be stupid," Phil said. "I'll go meet him with you, if that's OK."

Marvin nodded and looked at the two women. "We'll be right back. It shouldn't take long to say hello and good-bye to Big Mo."

Marvin and Phil were ushered into a private plush office at the rear of the bar. Big Mo weighed 300 pounds, and he was as bland and white as a ghost. One looks at his expensive custom black suit he is wearing with white button-down dress shirt, red silk tie. The lager diamond ring and gold watch probably with the money it cost you could buy a house for what the jewelry is worth that Big Mo is wearing.

Big Mo sitting behind an expensive mahogany desk with picture of Mayor John Lindsay and President Lyndon B. Johnson and Big Mo in the middle of both the Mayor and the President hanging on the wall behind him.

They walked in and saw a distinguished man sitting in the chair facing the desk, talking to Big Mo. Their conversation stopped when Marvin and Phil came in.

"Which one of you is Super Jew?" Big Mo asked.

"Me," Marvin said.

"I just want to talk with you."

Phil returned to the bar with the two women.

"I want you to meet Judge Meyers," Big Mo said.

Marvin shook hands with the Judge.

Big Mo turned his gaze back to the judge. "I'll take care of it. There should be no more problems after I talk with him."

"Thanks. Good-bye to both of you." The judge left.

"You made some name for yourself with that arrest on the train yesterday. You've got a future with the department. I take care of our own. I'm Jewish, too, and I can't count all the Jewish members of the department I made into bosses or put them into plush details on the job.

"If there's anything I can do for you, Marvin, just ask. I want you to be on my team."

"You have a cigarette?"

"No."

Big Mo opened a desk drawer and took out a half-empty box of cigarettes, then he took out a stack of hundred-dollar bills and set two hundred-dollar bills in the box of Camels. It's easy. We ask you for a cigarette, you give us the box of cigarettes, and we reward you by stuffing money inside the box. It's done all the time."

"Thank you."

"Never say that. Just take the box and never tell anyone what it is. I found out today you'll become a detective when you graduate form the Academy. I made a couple calls. And I'll get you onto the homicide squad if you want. The most-important thing is if you get into trouble call me. And we'll take care of it. If I need something, I'll call you. What kind of arrest did you make?"

"It was for rioting. How'd you know I'll be a detective after I graduate?"

"I'm the go-to guy if you want anything done in this city. I'm not bragging when I say I've got more info on politicians, judges, and cops to bring down the entire city. Did the idiot give you a hard time? If he did, I'll make a call. I can promise you he'll do big time in Attica prison."

"No, but thanks."

'I'll be a guardian angel looking out for you. Don't worry, Super Jew. You're on my team, and the means you can do almost anything. Like I said, if you need anything, call me, and we'll see what we can do."

They shook hands, and Marvin left the office looking for Phil and the two women. When Marvin met them at the bar, they asked what happened?

"Let's talk about something else besides Big Mo," Marvin said, looking at the two beautiful woman he saw a few minutes earlier. "What's your name?"

The gorgeous women in the business suit answered Marvin. "Betty. I come to New York City about three times a year on business. I'm a senior vice president of IBM in San Francisco. I'm staying at the Hotel Pierre in Manhattan. I have an expense account and would love to see a Broadway play, but we can't get out of Brooklyn with all these riots going on. We're stuck here!"

"Let's see what we can do."

"I'll be very impressed if you find a way to get the girls to Manhattan," Phil said.

"I'll be right back. I'll see what I can do to get them back to their hotel in Manhattan."

He walked away and knocked on Big Mo's door.

"Who there?"

"Super Jew."

"Come in. What's up?"

Marvin explained the problem about Betty and her girlfriend trying to get back to their hotel in Manhattan.

"Why don't you take them back?" Big Mo asked. "Maybe you'll get lucky and can spend the night with them."

"That's a great idea, but how can I do that when I'm waiting to be called into court for the arraignment?"

"Is that your only problem? We can solve that." He picked up the phone and called the bridgeman in the courthouse. "Hi, this is Big Mo. I've got officer Levey known as Super Jew here. He's doing me a favor. Lose his paperwork until he calls you. He'll call you when he's finished the assignment, he is doing for the commanding officer of the Brooklyn detective squad."

"Yeah, must be important assignment. I heard of Super Jew. OK, Big Mo. You and the commanding officer owe me one."

"Thanks." Big Mo hung up, then he called the desk officer at the Twenty-first Precinct. "I have one of your officers doing me a favor. Give him a police car, so he can get to Manhattan."

"OK. Big Mo. What's his name?" the desk officer asked.

"Super Jew."

"Send him over."

Big Mo hung up again. "You're got a car to use bring back the car when you're done at the Twenty-first Precinct and give the keys to the desk sergeant. Take the bridge officer's direct phone number when you're ready to go to court, call him and play the game that you're working for the commanding officer of the Brooklyn detective squad. He will never check."

He added. "Don't do anything with your dates that I wouldn't do.

They laughed.

Marvin went back to the bar and explained he had a police car to take the girls to their hotel.

"Can I come, too?" Phil asked.

"I couldn't pull off a miracle. I wasn't able to get approval for both of us to go to Manhattan."

Marvin and the two women left for the Twenty-first Precinct. When they arrived, he told the women to wait outside for him.

Marvin went into see the desk sergeant. "Hi, Sergeant. I'm Super Jew, and I'm here for a car."

"OK, Super Jew. You're a rookie? You're wearing a gray uniform. Do you need your uniform for whatever you're doing?"

"No."

"We've got a trench coat and floppy hat you can wear over that rookie uniform."

"That would be great."

The sergeant went into the locker room beside the desk and came out with a three-quarter-length black trench coat and a block floppy hat, handing them to Marvin.

"Big Mo must know what he's doing," the sergeant muttered.

He signed Marvin in and gave him the keys to an unmarked detective's car with a police radio. "Here are the keys. Your police car number is 1045. If they want you, the radio dispatcher will call you using that number. There's a sign on the dashboard with the number 1045 on it. Take the police car and use it and put the car back where you got it in the parking lot below the precinct. When will you be returning it?"

"I don't know."

"I'll keep the time and the date open."

Marvin walked out of the building wearing the trench coat and floppy hat. Betty and her girlfriend looked at him and laughed.

"I can tell, this will be a night that we will be thinking about of our life's," Betty said. "We were talking. If it is OK with you, we don't want you going right back to Brooklyn. It's too dangerous. Maybe you could stay the night with us?"

"You must've read my mind. I was thinking the same thing. We could stop and get something to eat."

"That won't be necessary. We have room service and an expense account."

"That sounds like a party. Let's make like a tree and leave."

They laughed, then Betty took his hand, and they walked to the unmarked police car and all three of them got into the car.

CHAPTER EIGHT

It's Party Time

The car's front seat was full of police equipment. Betty sat as close to Marvin as she could and put her left arm around him, pulling his head down for a long, hard kiss with plenty of tongue.

"I hope I'm included in this," her girlfriend said.

"I must've died and gone to heaven, Marvin said. "Of course, you're included."

All three got into the back seat and the women started removing their clothes. Marvin hugged them both, Betty opened his belt and tugged on his pants, but she could not pull them over his shoes.

Her girlfriend started kissing Marvin and placed his hands on her large breasts she put his erect cock into her mouth and started to blow him. Betty joined in an took turns sucking Marvin's dick.

Marvin laying on his back on the back seat of the police began moaning when Betty who is completely nude sat on Marvin face while her girlfriend is still blowing him. Marvin did his favorite porno star Johnny Holmes impersonation. He would have made Johnny Holmes's fans proud and stand up and cheer the way he made love to both women.

John Holmes was an actor who played in Almost 2,500 adult pornographic films. He died on March 13,1988 at the age of forty-three with a big smile on his face.

Marvin put his heart and soul into making love with both women for the next hour. He could not believe it, but he somehow, he stayed erect the entire time. The threesome did everything they could think of in the back seat of the police car.

Holy shit, Marvin thought. *We're in the police station parking lot in a police car. If I get caught making love with two women simultaneously, I'll either be fired or they'll give me another medal. This must be the best job in the world! I'm even getting overtime pay for this. These have been the best two days of my life.*

On the Way to the Hotel Pierre

As they drove, Betty said, "I had a great time in the parking lot with you two. I have to say, Marvin, you really are a Super Jew, but I have a commitment in San Francisco. If it's OK with you, I'll take your phone number. When I come to New York, I'll call you. I'm here at least four times a year on business. I really want to spend time with you when I'm in the city."

"Betty, I have to lay my cards on the table and admit I think I'm in love with you. Maybe I can come to California to spend time with you."

"That's impossible. I have a happy family in San Francisco, and you would complicate my life. You can't call me. I'll have to call you."

Marvin agreed and gave her his phone number. "I look forward to seeing you when you're in town.

"If it's OK with Betty," her girlfriend said, Maybe Super Jew and I can get together for dinner sometime? And when you're in city, Betty. I'm Always down for a three-way party with you and Super Jew."

"If Super Jew wants to be with you, Betty said, "I can deal with that. We can all meet for a party when I'm in town."

Marvin said, "I can definitely meet for a three-way party when you're in the city." Marvin exchanged telephone numbers with Betty girlfriend. Marvin gave Betty girlfriend his memo book and Betty's girlfriend wrote her name and telephone on a blank page in the memo book. Marvin read her name and said, "At least I know your name now." Its Mary Ellen. That's good to know when you call me at least I know who I'm taking too.

They all laughed.

Mary Ellen look at Marvin in an amazement. "You mean you made passionate love to me and you didn't even know my name?"

"Mary Ellen when we met at the Jury Box bar, I left to see Big Mo before we were introduced. But I can guarantee you this. I will remember you and Betty's name for

of my life."

They all got out of the police car in front of Mary Ellen's apartment house. Marvin gave Mary Ellen a goodbye kiss and Betty gave Mary Ellen a hug and said I'll call you when I get back to California.

Mary Ellen walked toward her apartment house.

"Let's continue this party when we're back at the hotel," Marvin said.

"What are you waiting for? Let's put the pedal to the metal and rush back to the hotel."

Marvin found the switches for the siren and emergency lights and turned them on, then he drove toward Manhattan passing red lights and driving on the wrong side of the street.

"Is this and emergency?" Betty asked.

"You bet. I'm about to make love to a beautiful woman."

She laughed and moved closer and put her arm around Marvin and gave him a kiss on his cheek.

They soon reached the Hotel Pierre. Marvin turned off the emergency lights and siren about five blocks away. When they pulled up to the hotel's front door, the doorman met them.

He took one look at the car and intuitively knew it was an unmarked police car. "Can I help you, Detective?"

"Yes. This is a big hard case." He looked down at his crotch, making Betty laugh. "We're on department business and have a room here."

"Is the woman in protective custody?"

"Yes, she is hiding out from her husband who would kill her if he knew what she just did. I can't get into any more details. But it's a federal case. Where can we park?"

"Use the VIP parking. I'll see about upgrading your room, too. Detective, all you must do is sign the police book, and the room's free, Along with meals and room service.

"Where's the book?"

"In the security room. All the staff there are retired or off-duty cops."

"Thank." He parked the car and went to the security room.

He met a retired third-grade detective who oversaw security for the hotel. "Are you Super Jew? We've been expecting you. Big Mo called and we know the deal. We made all the arrangements to make your stay at the Pierre hotel memorable. We upgraded your room to the Presidential suite. You will have your own butler and chef at your beckon call. We called Smitty, the cop who works on Broadway the theater district, he knows everybody. We got you and your friend tickets and the best seats in the house for the hit show *Hair*."

Marvin grinned. That show was the most-popular show on Broadway and just opened in April 1968. Tickets were impossible to get.

"To top off your day, we called Pete, the doorman at the Four Seasons the most elegant restaurant in the city, we made reservations for you and your party in the Oak Room for a late dinner. You don't have to worry about parking. You've got a police car. The best part is the whole night is on the arm."

"After the show and dinner, we called Steve Rubell the owner of Studio 54, and he said to meet Mario at the door. He'll usher you in without waiting on the long line.

Studio 54 was the old roundabout theater built in 1927 at 254 West fifty-fourth Street. It became the CBS radio studio from 1942-1966. Steve Rubell made it the most-popular nightclub in the world.

"I must be dreaming," Marvin said.

"No, Super Jew. This happens more often than you know."

The chief of security called for the bellhop to escort Marvin and his party to the Presidential suite in the penthouse. The Luxury suite took up the whole floor of the hotel.

As they arrived, they were met by their butler who is fully dress in a black tuxedo and tie. The Butler introduced himself. He bowed his head and stood up at attention and said "My name is James; I am here to serve all your needs. Is there any request that I can do for you?"

Marvin did not want the butler to see that he is still wearing his rookie police uniform under his rickety old detective trench coat and he wanted to make love to Betty as soon as he could.

"James is getting pretty late and what I like to do is give you the day off if it's OK with your boss?" Marvin said.

The chief of security smile and said, Super Jew I know what you and Betty are up too."

Marvin look at Betty they both smiled. Betty blushed. Marvin said, "chief you caught us."

The chief said. "James, they want to be Alone. You have the whole day off. See you tomorrow at 4:00 PM.

James bowed his head and said, "Thank you, Super Jew for the day off."

They all shook hands and the chief of security the bellhop and James left.

CHAPTER NINE

Showtime

The next morning, Marvin and Betty awoke after a long night of sex. It was eleven o'clock, and Marvin called the bridgeman at the courtroom.

"How am I doing with my arraignment?" He asked.

"Super Jew your arraignment paper is still lost. Looks like you're good until ten o'clock tomorrow night."

"That's great. I'll call you around nine."

"Remember my pound, Super Jew."

Marvin almost asked what that meant, then he remembered Pete telling him it was a five-dollar payment.

"Thanks, See you tomorrow."

After the call, Marvin and Betty wanted to dress and see Central Park, but Marvin still had only the trench coat and his recruit uniform. He called the security room and spoke to the chief about clothes.

"No problem," the chief said. "We've got a guy in the garment center who think he owns it. I'll introduce you to him. His name is Steve Sender. Anything you need, he can get. Do you need a suit, dress shirt and tie? Shoes? Give me your size, and we'll take care of it. They'll be delivered to your room."

Marvin gave him the information and hung up. "We have to stay here until my new suit arrives. Why don't we make passionate love while we are waiting for my new clothes to arrive?"

Betty, "sound like a plan."

Marvin held his hand out to Betty and lead her into the bedroom where they made love for the next forty-five minutes.

Betty ordered breakfast from their own gourmet chef.

An hour later, someone knocked on the door. It was the chief of security with Steve Sender with a suit, shoes and a medium-size cloth bag tied with a string.

Marvin let them in.

"Super Jew, I really wanted to meet you in person," Steve said. "It's great meeting a fellow Jew, especially a cop. If I can do anything for you, let me know I have a lot of important friends in high places in the city. I scratch their backs, and they scratch mine. I always get things done at the garment center. Try on this suit and see if it fits."

Marvin did and found it was a perfect fit.

Steve opened the bag and took out gold jewelry, a diamond gold pinky ring, and a Rolex black-face watch, the same model watch that James Bond wore in the movies. "Try on the ring and watch to see if they fit."

The ring fit OK though it was a little loose. The watch was loose. Marvin returned the watch to Steve.

Steve took a tool from the bag and adjusted the watch band. "Give me the ring." He took a small metal band from the bag and attached it to the inside of the ring. "Try them now."

"Wow! They fit perfectly."

"Super Jew, those are gifts. Happy birthday! Come by my office when you have a chance. I'm at 125 West Thirtieth Street on the sixth floor. If you hear the radio playing loud don't come in. It's a long story, but I hire airline stewardesses when they're on leave. I make love to them in my office. If that radio's playing loud come back another time."

"Got it. Thanks, Steve, for the gifts. If there's anything I can do for you, let me know."

"I've got to see the mayor now. It's about some bullshit about trucks parking on Fortieth Street and Seventh Avenue making deliveries to a large garment factory for some stupid reason their targeted by the meter maids and are getting parking tickets. See you later. Come by my office next Wednesday around two I have two beautiful airline stewardesses working that day looking to party."

"I'll try to make it. I hope I don't break my Rolex watch making love to the airline stewardesses." They all laugh.

Steve pick-up all his belonging and left.

"Super Jew," the security chief said. I must tell you that he's one of the wealthiest people in this city and owns half of Manhattan. He makes Big Mo look like a pauper, and he's Also one of the most-powerful people in the city. Looks like you hit it off well with him. I must go. If you two need anything, give me a call."

CHAPTER TEN

Let's Go Out and Party!

I'd better call my mother and tell her I'm OK, Marvin thought.

"Hi, Mom," he said. "I just wanted you to know I'm OK. I won't be home for at least another day."

"Marvin, I'm worried sick about you!" she said angrily. "Quit that job. You're getting all sort of phone calls from people I never heard of. One girl named Flo called four times. You got a call from a guy named Big Mo. Who he?"

"I made an arrest, and I'm tied up in court for another day. Mom don't worry about me. I'm safe. I'll be home sometime tomorrow. Whoever calls, just take a message, and I'll call them back when I'm home. I love you. I'll see you sometime tomorrow."

"Marvin, if your father were alive, he'd tell you to quit and come home. I need you. I don't want to get hurt."

"Love you, Mom." He hung up.

"Are you going home?" Betty asked.

"No. Let's start the party!"

Betty dressed in a 1960's outfit, with tall white go, go boots and a tie-died silk blouse and a truly short miniskirt.

Marvin could not take his eyes off Betty and said, "you are beautiful". Marvin put up his hand up and made a peace sign and said "Groovy!"

Marvin put on his custom-fitting three-button business suit, silver shirt with large collars, and skintight bell bottom pants. Marvin had to wear the only socks he had the black uniform socks from his police uniform. He added the new jewelry form Steve. He didn't know what to do with his service revolver. It wouldn't fit into his skintight pants pocket.

Betty helped, but it just would not fit. Finely, Marvin said, "I'll call the security chief to see if he has any ideas."

He called the Chief and explained the problem.

"You can put your revolver in the small of your back under your suit jacket, or I can bring you an off-duty holster that attaches to your belt. I'll need the holster back, just leave the holster in front of your door when you get back. I'll pick-up the holster when I get of duty at 8:00 AM."

"Thanks for the offer. I don't know what time we will be back from our night out. I'll try tucking the gun against my back under the jacket. Thanks Chief." He hung up and put gun behind his back under the waist belt of his pants, where it fit fine.

"When we dance, don't push the gun out of my back," he told Betty. "it would be very embarrassing if the gun fell to the dance floor."

They laughed.

"They went to the Four Seasons Restaurant at 99 East Fifty-second Street. When they drove to the front door, they met Pete the doorman.

"Are you Super Jew?" Pete asked. "We've been expecting you. Just park the police car. He met Betty in the lobby. They saw the spectacular décor and women dressed in expensive gowns and jewelry, with most men in tuxedos.

"I hope these meals are on the arm," Marvin said. "I've got only two-hundred bucks and a gun with me."

"I hope you don't need the gun to pay the bill."

"If things get bad, they'll call the cops. Then everything will be taken care of, I hop."

The maître d' came over. Super Jew, we have been expecting you. Big Mo made reservations for you. Do not worry about the bill. That has been taken care of. You just must sign the New York City Police Department book at the desk. We are supposed to hand that book to the department for reimbursement, but we have never done that. Have a good time. We are here to serve you. Please enjoy yourself."

He escorted them to the Oak Room, where all the movers and shakers in the city ate the most expensive dinner in the world and try to closed major business deals. Marvin looked around and saw famous movie stars, the most powerful politicians, TV stars that he knew from TV the popular TV shows.

Betty looked around the Oak Room and was impressed. "Super Jew look over at the next table, is that Vice-President Spiro Agnew?

"Yes, and you see who seating at Agnew's table" Lee Iacocca, Paul Newman and Joanne Woodward, Spencer Tracy and Katharine Hepburn."

Betty "I Always wanted to rub elbows with Paul Newman. I guess I got my wish."

"I'm doing pretty well for just two-days on the job," he said.

"It sure has been some two-days," Betty said. "I've been so busy; I haven't called my family yet. I will call them tomorrow from the hotel. It's long distance, and it's a hassle with all the coins you have to carry with you to make a long-distance call from a public pay phone.

The waiter walked up. "My name is Antonio, and I was told you are a friend of Big Mo. I am her to serve you and to make your dinner the best experience you have ever had. Your wish is my command."

He gave Betty the menu first then handed one to Marvin.

Marvin studied the prices and Almost laughed. This meal will cost more than a year's salary! He thought. The wine list included a 1965 Chateau Laffite listed at $10,000 per bottle, a Royal Demaria at $15,000 a bottle, a wine from the year 1775 Massandra at $43,000 a bottle, a bottle of Chateau Mouton Rothschild was on sale for $47,000. The most expensive bottle of all was a 1947 Chateau Cheval Bloc that went for astonishing $304,000 a bottle. Marvin idly wondered what a bottle of such expensive wine tastes like.

"May I suggest this?" Antonio pointed toward a bottle that went for $800 dollars a bottle.

Marvin looked at Betty. "That would be fine." When the waiter left to fetch the wine, Marvin added, "How bad can it be if it's eight hundred bucks a bottle?"

She laughed.

Antonio returned with the bottle and two Waterford crystal wine glasses, then he opened the bottle at the table. He gave Marvin a small sample.

"Please test the wine," Antonio said.

Marvin accepted the glass and wondered what to do, so he sipped the wine.

"I'll show you how to sample fine wine," Antonio said politely, "First, swish the wine in the glass. Hold the wine glass up to the light to see if the wine has legs. There should be a film left on the side of the glass. That what we call legs. You will also notice different colors of wine. Then take the sample glass of wine to your nose and open your mouth, taking a deep breath through your mouth, trying not to breathe through you nose. You should get the aroma of the wine."

"Now slip the wine and holding the sample wine to the tip of your tongue and press the wine to the roof of roof of your mouth and hold the wine there for about 5-seconds. That will give you the flavor of the wine."

"There are major differences of the taste of wine that you will notice. As you become connoisseur of wine you will enjoy great wines with your dinners."

Marvin did as instruct. "Wow. I really got the flavor that time. They certainly don't teach you how to taste fine wine at the Police Academy. Live and learn." He turned to Betty and added, "I don't think I'll be drinking Mogen David wine anymore."

All three of them laughed.

Marvin approved the wine, and Antonio poured two glasses for them.

"May I suggest dinner for you and Betty?" Antonio asked.

"What goes with a bottle of eight-hundred-dollar wine?" Marvin asked.

"Hamburger."

The laughed again.

"Super Jew, as you make a name for yourself, you will get better and better benefits. We have cops and city officials who qualify for Chateau Mouton Rothschild wine with their dinner."

"OK, Antonio. The way things are going, I'll be on that list next week. I'll leave the choice for dinner up to you."

Antonio nodded and left to place their order.

A few minutes later, four more waiters came to their table and began serving the couple.

Antonio supervised the serving process. "Would you like another bottle of wine?"

"I can't believe we finished the first one that fast," Marvin said.

"Water will be fine," Betty said.

"Don't worry about the bill, Antonio said. "it's been taken care of."

"OK," Marvin said. "Another bottle of fine wine would be great."

•••••••••••

One hour later, after finishing the best dinner Marvin and Betty ever had, they thanked Antonio for a fabulous meal.

"Where do I sign the city book?" Marvin asked. "Is the tip included?"

"The tip is usually included in the city book. Do not sign your real name. No one does that. The reason is a free dinner is a gray area. Who knows if you might get into trouble?

"Thanks for the information, Marvin said.

"It was nice meeting you, Super Jew. I hope to see you back here soon."

Marvin went into the office, where the clerk gave him a large ledger filled with printed names and signatures.

Marvin studied the names in the city book and laughed. He saw I.P. Daily, Mike Cock, Red Cross, the Three Stooges, and other, very funny names. It was clear no one used his or her real name when signing the ledger.

A quick check through the book showed that I.P.Daily came in about three time a week. Marvin wonder who is I.P.Daily he must be very important to come for dinner that offend.

Marvin took the pen and signed, *Mickey and Minnie Mouse.* The clerk took the ledger and gave it back to Marvin and said, "You can't use those names. They were here for lunch."

Marvin laughed. "Were Laurel and Hardy here today?"

"No."

"OK. I'll use those names."

The clerk returned the book, and Marvin signed before leaving with Betty to pick up the police car parked across the street.

They met Pete the doorman at the entrance.

"How was your dinner?" Pete asked.

"It was a great experience," Marvin said. "Thanks for everything, Pete."

"Remember to tell Big Mo we took good care of you. If you want, you can call me, and I'll see what I can do to get you and your friend in again."

"Thanks."

"Be safe. There are riots all over the city going on."

CHAPTER ELEVEN

Broadway Showtime

Marvin called the chief of security at the Hotel Pierre. "Where do I meet Smitty the cop?"

"He's waiting for you in front of the Biltmore Theater at 261 West Forty-Seventh Street. He has your tickets, the best seats in the house. You know how hard it is to get tickets to see *Hair*? The show just opened, and those tickets go for at least five hundred each!"

"Smitty has a parking place reserved for you on Forty-Seventh. I wish I were with you. Have a good time. I'll see you when you get up tomorrow."

Marvin and Betty walked to the police car, drove to the Biltmore, parked just outside the front of the theater, and met Smitty."

"Nice police car, Super Jew!" Smitty said.

They laughed.

Marvin is parked behind a new Rolls Royce limo, with a chauffeur inside. He noticed a line of parked limousines in front of the theater, all with chauffeurs.

"No problem," Smitty said. You can leave the car parked here. The other limos are required to have a driver in them."

Marvin and Betty got out of the police car.

"Thanks for the tickets, "Marvin said. "I don't know how to repay you."

"Consider it one of the benefits of your job. I got you seats on the First-row orchestra in the middle of the stage, the best seats in the house, so you two won't miss the nude scene."

"How was the Four Seasons? I go there all the time with friends and dates. Guess what name I use?"

"I hope it's not Laurel and Hardy."

Smitty laughed. "It's I.P.Daily."

All three laughed.

"When you're done with the show, I made reservations for you at Studio 54. Park the car on Fifty-Four street near Broadway by the corner, and no one will bother the police car. When you get there, see Darlan Rogers at the front door. He's in charge of security. You can't miss him. He's a perfect ten, about 230 pounds with a forty-eight-inch chest, thirty-two-inch waist, and eighteen-inch arms. He's about six-three, a light-light-skin black man in his late twenties. I know so much about him because we work-out together. We kid around all day when I'm with him. Darlan constantly tell me how he is in such good shape and can't wait to kick sand in my face when we go to the beach in Coney Island this summer."

"And wait to you see the most beautiful waiters, waitresses and bartenders in the whole-wide-world wearing the skimpiest outfits. The workers at Studio 54 become famous and very wealthy just by working there. I hope Betty don't leave you for the bartender'.

"Ok, Darlan will escort you into the club. Drinks and food are on the arm. Big Mo and I arranged this for you.

"Super Jew, you're making a name for yourself on the job. I almost feel jealous, but you'll soon learn we're all in the same boat. The blue code is. "All for one, and one for all. I know you only have two days on the job, and you're on overtime, but remember the blue code. When you see a cop in trouble, it's about helping him or her. If you stop his wife for a traffic ticket, it could be your wife next. Always remember the blue code.

"Have a great time. I might see you at Studio 54 when I'm off duty. I'd offer to buy you and Betty a drink, but the good news is, we don't pay for drinks."

Marvin and Betty entered the theater and took their seat. The show started, and the music and story line were the best Broadway show he ever saw.

••••••••••••

When they left the theater, it was total chaos outside with all the traffic and theater crowds. It seemed all the Broadway shows finished simultaneously.

Marvin tried to find Smitty, but he didn't see him. He and Betty walked through the maze of people and auto traffic to the police car. Marvin held the door open for her, then he got into the car.

"That was one great show," Marvin said. "Ready for the second half, partying at Studio 54?"

"I can't believe I'm not tired. I always wanted to go to Studio 54. It's a dream of mine, something on my bucket list."

"I'm here to fulfill your dreams. I keep thinking I've been dreaming for the last two days. I can't believe you're getting overtime pay for eating at the Four Seasons and seeing Hair and now partying at Studio 54. Maybe I should become a cop."

They laughed again. They gave each other a hug and a big long kiss. Betty said, "Let's party!"

CHAPTER TWELVE

Studio 54

Marvin parked the unmarked police car at the curb in front of Studio 54. A long line of parties stretched down the block from the club door, all waiting to get inside.

One look at the car, a blind person would know that it is an unmarked police car and people in line started dropping marijuana, guns, and drugs hopping not avoid arrest.

Darlan Rogers approached the car, "Super Jew, we've been expecting you. I saw your picture in the New York Post today. Big Mo called to say you and your date should get the VIP treatment. First, you can park your car around the corner on Eighth Avenue and Fifty-fourth Street. We don't want Studio 54 getting a bad reputation having a police car parked in front of our drug free place."

They laughed.

"Whatever you and your date see in the club, please don't take any police action. You're better off keeping it to yourself. You'd be in a lot more trouble than anyone you might arrest."

"Darlan, you have our word on that. What happens here, stays here."

"You guys will be in the private VIP room. You'll see many famous people: including politicians, sports figures, and movie stars. Don't be shocked by anything you see!"

"Do you want to park the car, or should I get one of the staff to move it? That's up to you."

"I'm already in over my head. Here are the keys.

Darlan escorted the couple into the studio.

Marvin and Betty were astonished by what they saw going on inside the club. It was the epicenter of drugs, sex and rock and roll. It was originally a CBS radio station before it was converted in a posh place to party! They were escorted to the VIP room on the second floor. In the elevator, they meet Truman Capote and Andy Warhol and two young, attractive couples. The moment the elevator door closed, the young couples lit a joint and passed it around.

Darlan watched Marvin and Betty when the joint reached them. He motioned Marvin to accept it and take a hit.

I never smoked a joint in my life, Marvin thought, *I don't even like smoking in general.* He took the joint and inhaled deeply. He instantly felt buzzed, happy, and giddy. "I'll probably get fired from the department for this, so I might as well have a good time."

Betty took the joint and took a puff. Having smoked marijuana before, she handled it like a pro.

When they handed the joint to Darlan, he politely declined. "I'll take you up on the offer once I'm off work. Mr. Warhol, are you having a good time?"

"Darlan, thanks for your help getting my group into Studio 54," Andy replied softly. "We need more ashtrays in the VIP room. Who's this cute guy with you?"

"These two are friends of Big Mo. This is Super Jew and his date, Betty."

"I remember now, I saw you in the newspaper today. Would you like to join our group to party? I always wanted to do a cop!" Andy smirked.

I'm being propositioned by a famous artist, Marvin thought. "Thanks for the invite Andy. We'd love to join your party, but I'll take a rain check on the lovemaking!"

The elevator door opened, and the group got out. Marvin and Betty caught the strong odor marijuana and the smoke was so thick, it formed a haze in the room. A large group was waiting to greet Andy and Truman. Andy introduced Super Jew to the crowd of incredibly famous, well-to-do partygoers. It was clear that sex and drugs were the themes for the night.

Marvin and Betty looked around and saw people from the movie, television, and politics they recognized. The large room had a dance floor, and a DJ played the top hits of 1968. Psychedelic lights and a large disco ball hung from the ceiling. Separated from the floor was a dimly lit enclosed balcony with three large, black-leather couches positioned in a U. A long glass table sat between them with a water pipe and four long hoses that ended in cigar holders so patrons could sample the marijuana. At the other end of the table was a razor blade and lines of white powder that people snorted with short straws. The group from the elevator sat on the three couches.

"I want Super Jew to feel at home," Andy announced. "We're had plenty of celebrities at our table, but never a real New York City cop before."

Marvin answered questions from the people around the table about the assassination of Martin Luther King, Jr. and the riots in the city. He assured them the city would be safe, while taking his turn smoking from the bong.

A gorgeous woman with long, red hair and crystal-blue eyes asked, "Super Jew, I saw your picture in the paper this morning and read the article about the ten arrests you made for murder. You're a hero. Can you tell us how you did that single-handedly?"

"I'd love to, but I'm under strict orders not to discuss the arrests until I testify before a grand jury."

"Which one of my artworks do you like best Marvin?" asked Andy Warhol.

"I like the Campbell's soup can the best. The chicken noodle soup is the best of all, that's what I have when I'm sick." Marvin answered as, marijuana smoke escaped from his mouth.

Everyone around the table giggled.

"Did you read *In Cold Blood*?" Truman Capote asked. "It's about the murder of a family of four in Kansas that divided the town."

"No, I haven't read it yet, but I promise I will."

Truman signaled a security guard standing near the entrance. "Please bring a copy of my book to the table."

"yes, sir."

The guard returned with a copy of *In Cold Blood*. Truman took out a pen and wrote "To Super Jew" then handed it to him. "I wrote my private phone number in there too, can I have yours?" Marvin gave it to him.

"If I ever need a favor, I'll call. You and Betty are invited to the biggest party of the century. My Black-and-White ball at the Plaza Hotel. It'll be the talk of the town. You're cute, maybe you can become my boy toy?"

Marvin put the hose from the water pipe down, "That's about the only thing I haven't done in the last two days. Let me think about it for a while."

"Perhaps you'd like to dance with me first?"

The band was playing *This Guy's in Love with you* by Herb Alpert.

"Thanks, Truman, but can't you see I've got a headache?"

Truman chuckled, "I'm not done with you. If I wanted, I could put out the story that you're gay, and the world would believe me!" Most of the news reporters in the city are gay. I'll bet you didn't know that J. Edgar Hoover, the director of the FBI, is gay too. He has private files on everybody, and he owes me a favor. He also was behind the assassination of President Kennedy! I'll let you in on a little secret. Hoover planned to pull the plug on the Kennedys. They got wind that he was going to go public with the dirt he had on them, so they were going to announce that Hoover was gay. He had no choice but to get rid of them." He frowned, "I've got a big mouth. Forget what I just said."

"I could call Hoover, and you'd be a police captain in a matter of weeks. I also bet I'll be kissing you at the Black-and-White ball."

"I'll bet you're full of shit, Truman. The director of the FBI is gay -right, you're smoking better stuff than I am."

"Super Jew, you have a bet," Truman said confidently. "The entire town will know you're gay, but that's a good thing. You'll get lots of support from civil rights organizations all over the city, even the world. All our gay friends are looking for a leader, and you'd fit the bill!"

"That's not going to happen. I won't kiss you until I get a huge diamond engagement ring." He held out his hand and pointed at his ring finger. The whole table cracked up.

"Super Jew, it looks like you're leaving me for Truman," Betty said frowning. "What does he have that I don't?"

"How about money, fame, and fortune!"

Betty removed her blouse and bra, "What about these?"

Marvin took one look at her breasts and said, "You win, you got me hook, line and sinker." He took her to a vacant couch and began making love to her in front of everyone.

"Go, Super Jew!" people chanted.

After intense lovemaking, Marvin and Betty dressed again and joined the group.

"Sorry Truman, I just got the urge to make love to a woman. Maybe after you buy me that expensive ring we could get together."

"You're such a cock teaser," Truman replied.

"Now I know what a woman feels like. If I play my cards right, I will wind up with a new car and an expensive house in the suburbs. All I have to do is string you on."

"I'll make a career of taking you to bed," interrupted Truman.

"I'm having fun teasing you."

"Super Jew, it's almost four in the morning," Betty said. "I'm high and tired, let's go back to the hotel."

"Ok, let's head out."

Marvin and Betty said good-bye to Truman, Andy and the others and then went to the elevator.

At the front door, they met Darlan Rogers again.

"You're the talk of the town, Super Jew. Walter Winchell, the newspaper, and radio gossip commentator was in the VIP room and saw you. He asked who you were. I wasn't going to tell him, but he said he'd call Truman Capote and find out anyway. He promised not to give your name on the air or in the newspapers, but it won't be hard to figure out it's you He said he would air the news that you're Truman's new boy toy!"

"Wow, I can't wait for my mother to find out I'm going out with Truman Capote.

"I hope Winchell doesn't mention my name. I've got a lot to lose, I'm happily married with a loving family in San Francisco." Betty realized.

"No one knows your name, Betty," Marvin assured her. "You're safe, I won't give your name to anyone. Everyone who knows me knows I'm not gay. I think my police career is over anyway, but what memories I've got from the last few days! Betty, I don't know about you, but I wouldn't change it for anything."

"Me either."

"Put a fork in me, I'm done." Marvin and Betty got the car and drove back to the hotel.

....

Next Morning, Day 3

Marvin and Betty were awakened by loud banging on the door. It was the chief of security for the Hotel Pierre. Marvin opened the door stark naked.

"Have you seen Walter Winchell's article in this morning's paper?" the security guard asked. "Super Jew, you've got calls from Big Mo and Steve Sender about it. They expect to hear from you soon."

Marvin took the newspaper from the man's hand and read the article.

"Looks like I made a name for myself in high society."

The article said a rookie cop with the initials SJ, who arrested ten murderers, was seen at Studio 54 Club's VIP room arm-in-arm with Truman Capote. It further stated that SJ was Truman's new boy toy.

"Who do you think told Winchell about you?" asked the chief. "I think it must have been Truman Capote himself."

"Chief, I'm not gay."

"That doesn't matter. The public thinks you are and so will the entire New York City Police Department"

Marvin looked back at Betty. "You're my witness, I'm not gay."

"Super Jew, the more I think about making love to you on the couch in Studio 54, the more I remember you screaming Truman's name."

They chuckled.

"The only person I care about is my mother, who'll eventually read this article. Excuse me, Chief. I need to call her now." Marvin dialed his mother's house, "Hello, Mom, there's a newspaper article by Walter

Winchell about me. It's not true, Mom. When I get home today, I'll explain everything."

"Are you OK, Marvin?" she asked. "Somebody named Madeline called from the mayor's office and left her phone number. She said she's the liaison between the mayor's office and a LGBT organization. She said they could help you. She wants to speak to you about the article."

"Mom, I'm fine. You don't have to worry about me. I'll see you later. Love you." He hung up, then dialed Big Mo's number.

"Hello, Big Mo?"

"You should've' told me you were gay Marvin."

"I'm not gay! Truman Capote made up that story because of a bet I made with him."

"You might not know this, but I'm gay. All my friends know it. We can use this opportunity to make you the leader of the gay community and create a gay union in the New York City Police Department. What do you think?"

"I'm all for civil rights for everyone, but how can I pull off being gay?"

"Don't worry, you'll have lots of support from the mayor and civil right groups around the country. Just leave it up to me. I've been thinking about starting a union for gays police officers for a while and even have a name for it—GOAL."

"What does that stand for?"

"Gay Officers' Achievement League, if you take on this assignment, I guaranteed you'll be promoted and will become a hero throughout the city. If you don't, I guaranteed you'll be fired by sundown. What do you say?"

"Just call me Mary."

Big Mo laughed, "I'll call the mayor and get back to you when you're in court. You just made the right choice."

"How will you pull off being gay?" Betty asked.

"This isn't meant as a joke," the chief said, "but I think you just bit off more than you can chew!"

"I'm boxed into a corner; I have to do what Big Mo wants. I'm probably screwed no matter what."

"What about calling Steve Sender?"

"I'll call him later today."

"I forgot to add that the bridgeman from court called. You have to be in criminal court by eleven o'clock today for the arraignment."

Marvin looked at his watch. It was 10:05 AM. "Looks like the party's over. Thanks for everything. I've got to get moving!"

"This has been some experience for me and my staff," the chief said. "Give me a call, and we'll have a room for you and Betty any time you need it. I wish both of you the best."

After he left, Marvin looked at Betty.

"I have to change into my rookie uniform and get to criminal court as fast as I can. The only problem is I can't remember what I locked the guy up for or what he looks like!"

"Don't worry, it'll all work out. After what we did in the last twenty-four hours, the arraignment will be a walk in the park."

"I have to be honest with you, I'm happily married, but I'll return to New York three or four time a year on IBM business. I'd love to get together with you again when I'm in town, but I have to call you. You can't call me."

Marvin took a piece of paper from his memo book and wrote his number down, handing the memo book to Betty. "I have to get to court. Call me when you're back home just to make sure you arrive safely."

"Good luck in court," she said in a soft, loving voice.

Marvin left the room dressed, but very disheveled.

·············

Court

Marvin, arriving at criminal court, walked past the officers waiting to be called for arraignment of their prisoners. He was startled to see beds, sleeping bags, and even beach chairs in the hall filled with cops waiting to go to court. He went to the arraignment office and approached the desk sergeant to sign in on the appearance sheet.

The sergeant looked at his signature and said, "We've been expecting you, Super Jew. You're the talk of the department. The bridge officer will call you in about ten minutes. Go find a seat in the police room. Big Mo and someone called Steve Sender called and asked me to tell you to call them as soon as possible."

"Did they say anything else?"

"They both read the article by Winchell, and they wanted you to know they'll be there for you."

Marvin lowered his voice and asked, "What did you hear about me?"

The desk sergeant lowered his voice too, "Besides making those great arrests, you're the first openly gay police officer on the New York City Police Department."

Looks like Truman won the bet, Marvin thought, *Let's see if this will benefit me like he said.* "Anything else come out about me?"

"Yeah, you're Truman Capote's boyfriend."

"What about the ten arrests I made for homicide?"

"That's old news. The whole department will remember you as the first openly gay police officer now. My son's gay, Super Jew, and we need more tolerance in this city and on the job. I'm sure you'll become our knight in shining armor."

In a proud, confident voice, Marvin said, "Sergeant, I'll do my best to achieve tolerance in the city."

"You make me proud!"

Marvin left and walked into the police room. He struck up a conversation with two cops sitting on an uncomfortable wooden bench.

"I'm Cary from the Sixty-first Precinct," one said. "I've got twelve years on the job."

"I'm Richard from the Seventeenth Precinct, and I've got over a year."

"How long have you been waiting to be called?" Marvin asked.

"I've been here ten hours," Cary said. "I'm starting to talk in Chinese."

"I'm going on my fourteenth hour," Richard said. "I'm really tired. How long have you been here? You look like hell!"

"I just got here; this is my first time arraigning a prisoner. What should I expect?"

"It's easy," Cary said. "When they call you into the courtroom, you sit in the first two rows on the right. You'll see other officers sitting there.

You wait to be called, and you go to the left side of the bench where the assistant DA stands. The right side's where the prisoner and the legal aid attorney stand. The court officer calls the bridge officer, who will swear you in that the arrest affidavit is true. The judge looks over the affidavit and sees what the prisoner's crimes are. He checks the guy's arrest record and determines if the man should be released on bail or put in jail. It takes less than two minutes. It's easy."

"Do they question you about the arrest?"

"No, they want to get rid of you as fast as they can."

"You mean to tell me I have to wait here for three days just to spend two minutes in front of a judge? That's crazy!"

"You don't get it, Marvin. You're on overtime. You're being paid time and a half for hanging out."

"That's the system," Richard added. "It's called collars for dollars. You can make a nice living locking up criminals. It's been like this as long as anyone can remember."

Marvin heard his name called.

"Who do you know to get called to court so fast?" Cary asked.

"Just lucky, I guess."

Marvin walked into the courtroom. Two court officers sat in the last row on the aisle, protecting the courtroom and able to apprehend any prisoner who tried to escape.

"Do you know where I should go to check in?"

"Hey, you're Super Jew, aren't you?"

"Yes."

"The mayor' office called and said to take care of you. Wow, it's nice to meet you. Take a seat in the front two rows on the right. I'll tell the bridgeman you're here."

The court officer walked over to the bridgeman sitting at the table before the judge. Marvin took a seat and noticed the court officer and bridgeman looking at him and still talking.

The bridgeman left the court officer and went to whisper to the judge. The judge called for a recess, and court adjourned. Everyone in the room stood as the judge walked out.

"Super Jew, come over here." The Bridgeman called out.

Marvin walked through the swinging gate and entered where the judge presides over the proceedings, the bench. And approach the bridgeman.

"Super Jew, I've heard you've had an amazing two days!" the bridgeman said with envy. "I've been assigned to this court for thirty-five years, and I never saw or heard of someone doing all the stuff you've done so far. First, the mayor's office called, and they're coming down to the court soon to talk to you. Secondly, Big Mo called and told me to take care of you and make sure everything goes well. Also, the FBI agent called and said, Hoover is taken a special interest in your case. Finally, Steve Sender called three times and needs you to call him back soon. To top it all off, we have newspaper reporters asking for an interview with you. It seems they want to know all about the first openly gay police officer! By the way, Flo, at the restaurant at the Academy is here and said she is worried sick over you. She wants to see you. I must ask, just how gay are you? How long have you been gay?

"I've only been gay for twelve hours," Marvin replies frowning.

The bridgeman was surprised, "You mean you aren't gay?"

"That's right, I lost a bet with Truman Capote."

"You're screwed if you aren't gay! If I can give you some advice, you better tell everyone you're gay and play along."

"I don't know anything about being gay. I don't know where to begin."

"The Honorable Judge Morgan is gay, and he's the judge you'll see for the arraignment. Just play the game, and it'll all work out. People have been looking for a leader of the gay community and you fit the bill!"

"Thanks."

"Super Jew, you owe me a pound. That's five dollars."

Marvin opened his wallet and took out two $100 bill he got from Big Mo. "Do you have any change?"

"Are you kidding? That's about what I take home after taxes every two weeks. You're one of a kind."

"How about I kiss you in front of the reporters instead?"

The two men laughed.

"When the court is called back in session, you'll be the first case. The prisoner is ready to plead guilty to disorderly conduct, which is a violation that carries a twenty-five dollar fine."

He then will pay the fine, fill-out some papers and walks out the door. Marvin, "You look like shit, why don't you go to the bathroom and freshen up?"

"Thanks," Marvin goes to the nearest bathroom.

When he returned, he found the judge's clerk waiting for him.

"Super Jew, Judge Morgan wants to speak to you in his chambers. Follow me."

Marvin followed the clerk to the front door beside the judge's bench and into the judge's chamber.

Why does the judge want to talk to me? Marvin wondered. *Maybe he found out what I've been doing for three days and will put me jail!*

They walked down a long hall toward an armed officer sitting on a chair guarding the door. They passed him and waved, as they walked into the judge's chambers.

Judge Morgan chambers is decorated in from floor to ceiling with bookcases filled with law books. Large oak desks with two chairs in front. with a bronze justice statue on top of the desk and legal papers pile neatly in a paper bin.

"I've been waiting for you, Super Jew, "Judge Morgan said. "I'm glad you came. I've spoken to Big Mo, Steve Senders, and the mayor about you. They all want you to be president of GOAL. I already spoke to my legal staff, and they'll draw up the papers to incorporate the organization. By next week, it'll be competed."

"However, you should know that currently any gay person can be arrested and charged under the state's sodomy laws. Under civil service law, you can't work in any federal, state, or city agency. In fact, you can't go into any licensed premises, like a bar without breaking the law! It's crazy, but you're classified mentally ill."

"We've been looking for a test case to change this crazy law. I promise you will not lose your job as a police officer with all the backing you're got. Plus, all the free legal services available to you if your case were to appear in court. You'll be a hero to the entire country, are you in?" asked the judge.

Bewildered Marvin thought, *I hope I can pull this off*, but said, "I'd be honored to be the president of GOAL, but I'll need a lot of help to the organization going. When do you want me to start?"

"Right now. You're the first president of GOAL!" He walked to his library shelves and removed a fake group of books. He pulled out a bottle of Jack Daniels, poured some into three glasses and added coke. He gave one to Marvin, and the clerk. He raised his glass and toasted, "TO GOAL may GOAL lead the way to tolerance in our city and the country!"

They all took a sip.

"Judge, I promise to do my best."

"We're all counting on you. I'll call you when the papers are ready. I want to invite you a date to big party we're throwing at the Stonewall Inn at 53 Christopher Street in Greenwich Village next Saturday at nine. I'll be in touch, I've got your phone number from the arrest report," added the Judge.

"I'll see if I can get off, but it'll be hard with all the riots in the city."

"I'll make a call," Judge Morgen said firmly, "You'll have Saturday off."

"Then I'll see you at the party, Judge."

After they finished their drinks, Marvin and the clerk left and returned to the courtroom. Marvin sat with the other officers waiting to be called.

The bridgeman called, "Officer Marvin Levey."

Marvin stood up and walked through the swinging gate into the center of the courtroom, standing beside the assistant DA to the left of the bench.

He shook hands and introduced himself to the female assistant DA, who was twenty-three with long, dark brunette hair, a slender build and stood five-feet-ten-inches.

In her white blouse and dark-blue business suit. She searched through hundreds of legal folders, looking for the one with Marvin's arrest report and affidavit. The stack of folders was at least a foot tall and did not seem to be in any order. Marvin offered to help.

While she looked, the judge continued arraigning the prisoner.

"What's the prisoner's name?" the ADA asked. "What was he arrested for."

"I don't have a clue; I don't even remember what he looks like."

"You must be kidding," she said softly. "The prisoner's standing beside his lawyer. Look at him, does he seem familiar?"

"No, I'm serious. I don't remember what I arrested him for."

"Check your police memo book. You should have all the details in there."

Marvin felt his pockets and remembered he did not have it. "I don't have my memo book with me."

"Don't say another work. I'll take care of the arraignment and get you out of here as fast as I can."

The ADA made a motion to approach the bench. Both lawyers and the stenographer walked up to the bench. The judge motioned Marvin to come forward too,

"Stenographer," the judge said, "This is off the record. Super Jew, I see you charged the defendant with rioting and resisting arrest. If he in any way gave you a hard time, I'll throw the book at him and put him away for seven years. Just say the word, and he'll go to jail."

"Judge, I believe the prisoner has some redeeming qualities and could become a productive member of society. Let's give him a break. I'll go along with ADA's plea deal. I feel a fine would be a sufficient penalty without prisoner time."

"The people will accept a plea deal for disorderly conduct," the ADA said.

"Super Jew," Judge Morgan said, "You have a soft heart. The court will go along with the fine. See if the defendant has ten dollars."

The legal aid attorney went to the prisoner and told him about the deal. He asked the man to accept the deal and added that the cop was willing to go to bat for him and wanted to give him a break. "If you don't accept this deal, you're looking at seven years in prison!"

The prisoner checked his pockets and came up with $6.37 and his lucky rabbit's foot keyring. "That's all the money I have in the world. I don't have a job, I'm on welfare."

"I'll see if the judge will accept six dollars for the fine."

The attorney approached the bench and explained the situation.

Let's get the hell out of here, accept the deal, Marvin thought. Turning to the ADA, he said, "Six dollars is OK with me, since he doesn't seem to be very lucky, why not take the rabbit's foot too as part of the deal."

The ADA nodded.

In a bored voice, the judge said, "I accept, the fine is six dollars and thirty-seven cents and the lucky rabbit foot keychain."

The participants returned to their places and stood while the judge gave his standard guilty speech, something he said hundreds of times.

"Are you pleading guilty to disorderly conduct?"

"Yes," the prisoner replied.

"Did anyone threaten you or promise you any deals?"

The legal aid attorney whispered, "Say no."

"No."

After the judge read the two pages of the guilty plea procedure, he sentenced the prisoner to pay $6.37 cents and to forfeit his lucky rabbit's foot keychain. Everyone in the courtroom laughed.

The prisoner was given a sentencing form to sign, then he was released.

He went to the table to thank Marvin. "Super Jew, thanks man, for not pushing for jail time. The judge looked ready to make an example of me. I promise I will straighten out my life. I needed this to open my eyes. I might be able to help you solve some major crimes in the city. I have information that they convicted the wrong guy for the Lover's Lane murder. The real killer is Lu-Lu Boy James. Can you give me a piece of paper?"

Marvin tore a piece of paper from a notebook on the table and handed it to him.

"He's on the loose in Queens." He said while writing down the name and address where he could be found. "I've got more information about unsolved crimes in Brooklyn and Queens too. If I get caught doing something stupid, I'll call you. I expect you to give me a break."

"I can't promise to get you off, but I'll do my best. Let's see if the information is true first, give me your phone number. If it pans out, maybe I can help get you a job."

"Remember one hand washes the other, you help me, and I'll help you!"

They shook hands to seal the deal.

"This could be the start of a wonderful friendship," Marvin left the man to pay his fine and turned to the judge, who gave him a wink.

Marvin left the courtroom and returned to the police room. Cary and Richard were still waiting for their cases to be called.

"Boy, you really got called quickly, with all the riots going on we must be arresting half the city. Have you heard about the two officers stomped to death by a mob in Brooklyn? They surrounded the police car and pulled them out and killed them!"

"We've been here for twenty hours," Richard said. "I'd like to get the hell out of here. They need us out there. We're wasting time here. We could be doing our jobs. I can see us sitting here another twelve hours!"

"I guess I was lucky to get called so fast," Marvin laughed. "What do I do to get of here now?"

"Go in and see the sergeant. Tell him the deposition and the date you have to come back for court."

"The prisoner pleaded guilty; do I have to come back?"

"Didn't they teach you anything in the Academy?" Richard asked. "You're done. Just tell the sergeant the deposition is guilty, sign out, and go back to your command. When you get back, see the desk lieutenant, and tell him about the deposition before you sign out. You're off the clock."

"What do you mean, I'm off the clock?"

"Your overtime is over. You're officially off duty. Get back as soon as possible to your command. You get paid portal to portal which is Forty-five minutes to get back to your command whether you're back to command in ten minutes or an or Two-hours."

They said good-bye and told each other to stay safe.

Marvin went into the police office and met the sergeant to sign out of court and returned to his command.

"Super Jew, you're done already?" the sergeant asked.

"The prisoner pleaded guilty and was fined a whopping six dollars and thirty-seven cent plus his lucky rabbit's foot keychain."

"You're kidding."

"It's true."

"I called my son and told him I met you. He said he's proud of all you're doing for the gay community and you're in his prayers. He'd love to meet you."

"Thank him for me. When things calm down, maybe he'll come to one of our GOAL meetings, and I can say hi."

"I'll ask him" The sergeant signed Marvin out and told him he had forty-five minutes to return to his command at the Academy.

"How much time does the department give you if you're in a different borough?"

"The rule is, if you're in the same borough as your command that dismissed you from your detail, you back to your command. The contract states the job gives you forty-five minutes to get there."

"So if you're on parade or a detail in another borough, the job one hour and fifteen minutes to get back to your command. That's called portal to portal. It's in the contract, if you come in late, you're on your own time. Those are the rules. I have a message for you from Big Mo, Steve Sender, and Flo. They all want you to call as soon as possible."

"Got it, thanks Sergeant. I'll call them when I'm home. I'm too tired to talk to anyone right now."

Marvin went to his unmarked car. He had to return it to the Twenty-first Precinct in Brooklyn, and then hail a cab to the Academy on Twentieth Street in Manhattan. It would take him at least two hours.

CHAPTER FOURTEEN

Back to Command

When Marvin left the courthouse, he heard emergency sirens. He saw and smelled smoke in the air. Twenty police vans were lined up filled with rioters who'd been arrested and were waiting to be arraigned in court.

The city's coming apart at the seams, he thought. *I'd better get back and join my fellow officers. The party's over!* He started the unmarked car, turned on the lights and siren, and raced down the street to the Twenty-first Precinct, where he was headquartered.

As he passed a large group of rioters, the was rioters carrying couches, TV sets, shoes and believe it or not a one group was rolling a large heavy safe down the street.

Marvin floored the accelerator and sped toward the crowd. As he approached, the rioters pelted his car with rocks, bottles, and gunshots. One bullet shattered the front window. Marvin had trouble seeing through the broken glass.

I need to get the hell out of here, my life's in jeopardy and I'm in danger, he realized. *I can use deadly physical force!*

He set his gun in his lap, running over rioters and emptying the gun into the crowd. He knew he didn't dare stop, because they'd capture him and beat him to death like the other police officers who'd been caught.

He drove over one hundred miles per hour, like someone in a demolition derby. He bounced off parked cars and finally crashed into a wall. The car came to a sudden stop. Dazed, he realized he was in shock. When he woke up a few seconds later, he saw the mob running toward him.

Marvin took cover behind a parked car in front of his police car, which was burning, filling the street with dark heavy smoke, and making it hard to see. He checked his belt and determined he had only eighteen bullets left. If he got into a gun battle, he had to use ammo sparingly. Maybe he could hide somewhere, so the mob would not locate him. He found an alley between buildings with a large Dempster Dumpster. *What do I have to lose?* He wondered.

Marvin limped to the Dumpster and dived in on top of the garbage. A horrid smell assaulted him, as he closed the cover. He held the lid open just enough to be able to still see out.

The mob arrived quickly and looked around.

"Where the hell are the cops? They couldn't have gone far. I want to kill those sons of a bitches! I want to waste them with the guns we took off the dead cops yesterday. We'll get their money and jewelry, and more importantly, their guns and their police shields," one of the rioters yelled.

"Look for cops!" someone else shouted. "If we find 'them, we'll kill 'them. They must be hiding."

Marvin's gun was cocked and ready in his right hand. His heart was pounding, and he was sweating profusely. He thought his life was over, so he prayed for God's help.

A pair of rioters came to the dumpster and placed their hands on the lid ready to raise it. Right then however, police sirens sounded, coming closer and closer and the sound of the sirens became louder and louder.

I might as well empty my gun at the rioters, Marvin decided, *they'll kill be anyway, at least the gunshots will bring the cops to me quicker!*

He jumped up and threw the lid open, at the same time firing at the two rioters. A police car screeched to a halt just as Marvin opened fire on of the rioters milling around. He killed four of them instantly as six other police cars arrived.

of the mob fled!

Marvin climbed out of the dumpster covered with garbage and smelling like rotten food, dog shit and dead fish. "On the job!" he shouted. "Don't shoot!"

Several officers ran toward him.

"Are you all right?" one asked.

"Thanks a lot, you guys. You saved my life. These were the asses who stomped two police offers to death yesterday!"

"How do you know that?" the sergeant asked.

Marvin bent down and picked up a New York City police service revolver and opened the cylinder. Four spent shells lay inside, with two live rounds. He dumped out all six and handed the gun and shells to the sergeant.

"I bet that's one of the hero cop's guns the rioters killed yesterday. I overheard them bragging about killing the cops!"

"We can easily check that out using the serial number of the gun. It won't pay to get that rookie uniform cleaned. We'll get you a blue one. You deserve it, what's your name, Officer?" asked the sergeant.

"They call me Super Jew; I'm assigned to the Police Academy. Maybe someday I'll get back there and learn what the jobs all about."

"I've heard of you. You've already got some reputation. I'm proud to meet you. I'll write this shooting up, so you're awarded the New York City Police Department's Medal of Honor! It doesn't get any higher."

He told Super Jew to climb into the back of his cruiser and then drove him to the Twenty-first Precinct to be interviewed by the duty captain and the homicide detectives.

When they arrived, they were mobbed by reporters who wanted to interview Super Jew. Marvin didn't want to talk to anyone until he cleaned himself up. As the sergeant drove around to avoid the press, reporters spilled into the street and banged on the windows, acting as badly as the rioters Marvin just escaped from.

"Stop the car, let me out to talk to them."

"Driver stop the car," the sergeant said.

Marvin got out and faced the reporters. "Look guy, I'd like to wash up before I get interviewed, ok?"

They immediately pelted him with questions about the recent shootout.

"How come you're covered with garbage and smell like dog shit?" a reporter asked.

Marvin explained how he hid in a dumpster, only to jump up and shoot at the very rioters who had killed the two police officers with their own guns!

They wrote furiously, knowing the story would-be front-page material the next day.

"Look," Marvin finally said, "I have to go inside the precinct and be interviewed by the detectives. More importantly, I have to get out of this stinking uniform."

"Super Jew, you look perfect to me," Cindy Sears, a beautiful TV reporter said, handing him her card. "Give me a call."

Marvin instantly recognized her from WNBC, Channel 4. He watched that channel because of her. He'd fell in love with her years earlier and actually dreamed that one day he would meet her and married her.

"I'd love to call you if I ever get a day off. We could go out and get something to eat," Marvin said shyly.

Cindy replied quickly, "Super Jew, I'd love go out with you."

Pinch me, I must be dreaming. "Cindy, you'll be the first call I make when I get that day off."

Captain Katz, the commanding officer of the Twenty-first Precinct, ushered Marvin through the doors. "Super Jew, you might not believe this, but the police commissioner, Mayor Lindsay, Big Mo, Steve Sender and the gay community leaders are all waiting for you inside. By the way, you look and smell like shit."

Marvin walked into the building and was immediately led to the captain's office to meet the officials.

"I want to speak with Super Jew for a moment," Mayor Lindsay said.

Everyone but the mayor, the commissioner, and Marvin left the office.

"Super Jew, you're some piece of work," the mayor said. "We all know what you did in the last couple of days-you stayed with that woman in the Pierre Hotel for free, saw Broadway shows for free, and went to the Four Seasons to eat like a king—all on city time. You've got serious balls. To top it all off, you aren't even gay!

"If you weren't a hero to the press and the public, I'd fire you in a heartbeat! You're in such a superior position, I can't fire you. Instead, I have to promote you to third-grade detective and give you a pay raise."

"The mayor's right," the police commissioner said. "Since we can't fire you, we have to make you a hero and promote you to detective. You'll be the first rookie officer in the history of the New York City Police Department to make detective after only three days on the job. You'll also be the first openly gay officer in the department's history. However, you must agree to maintain the charade of being gay to and become the president of the new gay organization called GOAL. That's politically correct for the city and country. If you don't agree, we'll fire you for what you did while being paid overtime!"

Marvin realized he didn't have many options, "Just call me Mary, I agree. I'll do my best to start GOAL, but I'm not doing it to save my job. I want to help bring civil rights to everyone. What about the public moral laws that make being gay illegal? I could be arrested for being mentally ill and carrying a gun!"

"That's the whole point," commissioner said. "That's the purpose, to get rid of any law that says being gay is a crime! You are our test case for changing the law. GOAL will used as the vehicle to change that law and will bring various groups together. What do you think of that!"

"I'm on board with it. I believe I can pull off being gay and will fool most people."

"You make us proud, Super Jew," the mayor said. "You're a great American, but I have to tell you, you look and smell like dog shit."

They all nodded their heads and walked from the office to meet the press for the formal announcement of his promotion.

"How about you let me wash up before I meet the press again?"

"I want you looking like a tough hero," the mayor snapped. "Dog shit makes you look the part."

"It makes me feel and smell like shit."

They laughed and were soon in the press room behind the podium in front of a sea of reporters and press representatives. Cindy was there too. Marvin couldn't take his eyes off of her. He never felt such total love for a woman before.

How can I announce I'm gay in front of Cindy? He wondered.

"I have the distinct honor of announcing rookie cop Marvin Levey, better known as Super Jew, will be promoted to third-grade detective immediately for his distinguished work during his three-day career as a rookie New York City Police officer! He has already made ten homicide arrest and shot and killed four rioters who murdered two heroic NYPD police officers yesterday!" the mayor announced loudly.

He turned toward Marvin. "You've had some three days as a rookie cop!" He then turned back to the press. "I just want the people of New York City and the country to know that he is also announcing that he's gay and will be the president of a new organization called Gay Officers Achievement League, knows as GOAL. He has the support of the City of New York. He wants all gay NYPD officers to come out and join GOAL. As of today, there will be no repercussions for any officer who admits he or she is gay."

He signaled the police commissioner and Marvin to step to the podium. The commissioner took a detective's shield from his pocket. "Marvin Levey, stand at attention." He pinned the new shield to the front of Marvin's dirty, smelly rookie jacket. Members of the Twenty-first Precinct and the entire press core applauded.

"Super Jew, how do you feel about being the first openly gay officer." Asked a reporter from the *New York Times*.

"I'm glad you asked," Marvin said. "I'm grateful for the support from the mayor, the police commissioner, and the City of New York. Most importantly, I'm grateful to Truman Capote, who pledged a donation of $100,000 to start GOAL in my quest to obtain civil rights for all New York's gay police officers."

"When and where did Mr. Capote make such a pledge?" the reporter continued.

"Over drinks at Studio 54 he hugged me and said sweet nothings in my ear. Truman said he would make the official announcement of his donation at his annual Black-and White ball at the Plaza Hotel next week, which I will attend."

When he finds out, he'll know I won our bet, Marvin thought. *There's no way he can back out of his donation now.*

"Super Jew, could you please tell us how you solved the murder case of the two police officers?" the reporter from the *New York Post* asked.

"Those murderers chased me and wanted to shoot me and stomp me to death. They screamed and was immensely proud of what they did killing those two cops by stomping them to death, yesterday! I had no choice but to hide in dumpster. When the opportunity arose, I emptied my service revolver into those murderers and recovered the stolen police officer's guns that rioters took from the hero cops."

Super Jew," Cindy from WNBC said, "I think I have a crush on you, are you planning to call me so we can have our date?"

This could blow the entire charade of me being gay, Marvin thought. He turned red, blushing before the press, turned to Cindy and said, "If I weren't gay, you'd be the first woman I'd marry in a heartbeat. I'll make a deal with you. We'll have our date and see what happens."

"Ok, Super Jew, it's a date. I never had this feeling about anyone before. I feel safe with you."

The mayor took the microphone again. "I think Super Jew deserves a couple days off. Detective, as of now, you don't have to report to work for two days. You're off duty. I hope you and Cindy can spend some time together and become good friends."

"Thank you, Sir."

Marvin walked toward Cindy, "Let me wash up, and then we can have a late dinner date."

"I have to file my report at the station, then I'm off too. Where should I meet you?"

Marvin thought for a moment, "Meet me at the Four Seasons in two hours."

The other members of the press were surprised.

"Detective," the mayor said, "You don't make much more than a police officer. You might have to take a loan to pay for a meal there!"

"Super Jew, we don't have to go there, how about we go to Katz's Delicatessen instead. I'm fine with Dutch treat too." Cindy smiled.

"I think it'll be cheaper if we go to the Four Seasons."

"You mean the meal will be free?"

"You should be a detective," Marvin said smiling.

"I'll meet you by the fountain in the lobby at ten." Marvin checked the clock over the door and realized it was already 6:30. He had to get moving, as he still had to make a few calls."

Big Mo walked into the room. "Super Jew, I'd shake your hand, but I'm afraid to touch it since you just climbed out of a dumpster!" he laughed. "What's up with that reporter, Cindy? Are you seriously going out with her?"

"Yes, in fact I was going to ask you to make arrangements for us to have dinner at the Four Seasons tonight."

"You could blow the whole gay thing, but what the hell I'll make a call. You two have a great time, and don't do anything I wouldn't do."

Four Seasons Two Dinners in Two Nights

Marvin, after borrowing a razor, cleaned up in the Twenty-first Precinct and put on the same suit he wore the previous night. He met Pete the doorman at the Four Seasons.

"Hey, Super Jew, this is becoming a habit. You're here two days in a row. Big Mo called and took care of everything. You and your date enjoy yourselves. You've got an upgrade for dinner with wine tonight. That's a record time for getting an upgrade too. You're on the same level as the mayor now. By the way, we at the Four Seasons what to congratulate you on your promotion to detective!"

"Thanks Pete, for the upgrade."

Cindy walked up, "Super Jew, I had a bet with the anchor at WNBC that you wouldn't show up."

"I hope you didn't bet too much money."

All three laughed.

"I watch you all the time on TV," Pete said. "I think you're very professional. Most importantly, you're very cute. Can I take a picture with you? I have a photo album with all the movers and shakers in the city, and I'd love to include you."

"Sure Pete."

"Can I get in the picture too," Marvin asked.

"Sure," Pete agreed. He went into the lobby and came back with a Konica camera. He asked a driver, who was waiting for a patron to come out, to take the picture by the Four Seasons sign.

Marvin and Cindy went inside and were immediately met by the maître d'.

"Super Jew, we've happy to see you again," he said. "Big Mo made the reservations for you and Miss Cindy. Don't worry about the bill, it will be taken care of. Super Jew, we've upgraded you to Gold Card that will entitle you to the most expensive and elite private clubs, hotels, and restaurants around the world. The benefits allow you to bypass lines, enjoy exclusive entrees and our most-expensive wines. Only the president and other heads of state are at our highest level—Platinum. If you achieve that status, I'll wear a dress, makeup and a woman's wig to work, and kiss you in front of this building!"

"This is only my first week on the job. I've already did more as a rookie than most cops do in their entire careers. Get ready to be kissed!"

After sharing a chuckle, Marvin and Cindy were escorted to their table in the corner facing the oak room. It seemed like an army of waiters, supervised by Antonio, the headwaiter, came over and began serving them.

"Super Jew, we're here to serve you and Miss Cindy. We are at your becking, call. The owner will come to meet you and give you your new gold card, then all of us will toast you and sing *Let the Good Times Roll.* You will be expected to make a short speech and the press will take your picture! You'll be the talk of the town."

Marvin looked at Cindy, "Just another day of police work. Can you deal with this? If not, we can leave. I don't know if you want your name in the press with me?"

"It's been an exciting date already. I'll stick by your side. I want to witness this."

"Thanks, Cindy," then asked Antonio, "Could you bring me a phone, I want to call my mother."

One of the waiters immediately came over with a fancy white princess phone and plugged it into a nearby telephone wall jack.

"Hi, mom, I just wanted to tell you I'm OK, and I've been promoted to detective."

"I know about the promotion and all the things you did. It's all over the TV and newspapers. Marvin, you're some piece of work! I know you aren't gay. How did the media get that story?"

"It's a long story, Mom," he said in a lower voice. "Just play along until I get home, then I'll explain it all to you."

"I have to know, are you gay?"

"I can't talk now," he whispered. "But the answer is no."

"Thank God! You have so many calls, I'm running out of paper to write them all down. You have ladies calling you, one from San Francisco. They're all worried about you."

I'll take care of the calls when I get home, Mom, I love you."

"Marvin, please be careful. You're all I've got."

He hung up.

A moment later the owner of the Four Seasons and a group of TV and newspaper reporters walked over and introduced themselves.

"Super Jew," the owner said, "It's a pleasure to meet you and Miss Cindy. I want to bestow upon you the gold card, which makes you a member of one of the most-elite clubs in the world." He handed Marvin a gold metal card with the name *Detective Marvin Levey (Super Jew)* embossed on it.

The reporters took photographs and wrote stories for the 11:00 news. The patrons in the room stood up to toast Marvin and sang *Let the Good Times Roll.*

After the song, Marvin was handed a microphone. He lifted his glass of expensive champagne and toasted the New York City Police Department. "I want to thank New York City and the police department for giving me this opportunity to protect and serve the people of this great city. I promise I will help stop the riots and return this city to a safe place to live. I want to also thank Jim, the owner of the Four Seasons, for the honor of being installed into the most-prestigious clubs in the world, thank you Jim."

He glanced at Cindy and saw her smiling proudly. She winked at him.

Marvin turned to the patrons, as the room erupted into a round of applause. They raised their glasses and toasted him.

"Super Jew," an NBC reporter asked, "You shot and killed scores of rioters in the last two days. How can you go out and celebrate after that?"

"If I didn't take police action, I wouldn't be here tonight. If those muggers escaped, they'd be free to mug or kill other people's loved ones. Guys, I'm here to enjoy my day off, and all those criminal cases are being investigated. I can't go into detail at this time."

"Is Cindy your date?" a CBS reporter asked. "Are you two going out?"

Marvin peeked at her and gave her a big smile, "We just met and hopefully will become very good friends, and I need to get back to her, so I need to end our discussion."

With a final round of applause, the conference ended. The reporters left, and the room soon returned to normal.

In a jovial mood, Marvin said, "I'm glad that's over with those pushy news reporters."

"I hate to give you bad news, but I'm a reporter, too."

"I guess I have to be careful what I say around you,"

"Super Jew, we have a private relationship, whatever we do together is between us."

"Ok, Cindy, let me test you on that. Whatever I say is a secret between us. I've fallen in love with you and want to be with you for of my life!"

"I feel the same way about you, I've never felt this way about anyone before. Why don't we finish our dinner and go to my place on the Upper East Side?"

"I'm the luckiest man on the face of the earth, let's eat and leave."

He signaled Antonio, "I'm deeply sorry, but have to rush out of here. We have an important affair to go to on the Upper East Side."

Cindy and Marvin kissed and then gave out with a big laugh.

"Super Jew, we can get you out of here in fifteen minutes, well fed. I can package any food that you can't finish to take home with you. I give you a present of a bottle our brand of fine wine that sells for $60,000 to take home with you and Cindy. If you promise not to tell my boss." He was good as his word. Marvin and Cindy had the best dinner and wine they ever ate in such a short time They rushed to finish so they could leave and go to Cindy's apartment.

Antonio came over, "Super Jew, you just broke the record here. You two gobbled down an $800 dinner and finished a half of bottle of $62,500 Rothschild wine!"

"So sorry, we have a pressing engagement at Cindy's place!"

"I wish I was going with you." Antonio replied, "I know what you're up to, think about me on the up stroke."

Marvin drove to Cindy's apartment passing red lights and waving around heavy traffic, knowing he would not get a summons. They arrived at her condo and parked in front of the building. The doorman met them and allowed them to enter the luxury high-rise residential building. Cindy said, "Good evening, Walter."

"Are you Super Jew," he asked. "The detective I saw on the six-o-clock news?"

"Yeah, that's me."

"I want to thank you for what you've done to keep this city safe with all the riots going on. I'm scared the rioters will come this way. How would I protect the residents?"

"If those asses come here, call me at Cindy's," Marvin replied in a confident voice. "It would be a pleasure to take care of them."

"Thanks!"

Marvin and Cindy entered the elevator, and she pushed the button for the penthouse. His arms went around her. She responded with a warm kiss and pressed her hand against his butt, pushing him closer so she could rub her body against his. He rubbed his chest against her breasts.

The elevator stopped, and door opened at the fourteenth floor. They were still kissing when a priest tried to enter the elevator. After taking one look at the couple, he said, "You two need to come to church for confession."

They opened their eyes seeing the priest in his vestments and apologized. The priest entered the elevator. Then the priest asked. "Aren't you the detective they call Super Jew, and aren't you the TV news anchor?"

"Yes, we are."

"Then what you two are doing in the elevator makes sense."

"How's that?" Marvin asked.

"You're Jewish, and she's part of the lying media! Why don't two get a hotel room?"

They all laughed until the elevator reached the penthouse floor. The priest remained on the elevator, saying good-by to Cindy and Marvin. They quickly opened the door and started removing their clothes, as Cindy led the way to her bedroom. On the walls were original paintings, one by Andy Warhol and on her nightstand was Capote's *In Cold Blood.*

The room was furnished with most expensive items Marvin had ever seen. The bed was by designed by Abdolhay Parnian with a solid gold headboard. The end table was handcrafted in the 1700's by Thomas Tuffy.

Marvin thought, *this bedroom set alone is worth a million bucks.*

While he and Cindy were kissing, touching, and nibbling, getting each other more and more excited. *I'd better do my best when I make love to Cindy. I just hit a homerun. I want to make her as satisfied and happy as I can.*

While he rushed to the bed, Cindy stepped on the clothes Marvin tossed on the floor and felt something give.

"I think I bent your new detective shield," she giggled.

"That's ok, whenever I put it on, I'll be a reminder of this moment." *I might as well do my Johnny Holmes impersonation,* he thought.

They got into bed nude, and Marvin did his best impersonate of porno actor Johnny Holmes. Marvin could have won an Academy Award for best supporting actor in a porno movie.

They made love to Cindy eight times that night. Marvin marveled at his stamina!

•••••••••••

When they awoke at ten o'clock the next morning, Cindy said, "That was the best night of my live, I'm not even tired!"

"Me either."

Marvin hugged her, and they made love for the ninth time that day.

"Let me make us some breakfast," Cindy said.

"Do you have nuts, figs and coffee? That's what I eat most day for breakfast."

"I have walnuts and fruit, will that do?"

Marvin got out of bed and dressed before sitting at the kitchen counter Cindy came over and they hugged and kissed some more.

"I have to ask how you can afford to live in a place like this."

"Cindy Sears is my stage name; my real name is Elizabeth Rockefeller. Nelson Rockefeller is my uncle."

"You've got to be shitting me, you're a Rockefeller!"

"You won't hold it against me, will you?"

"I've been in love with you well before I found out you were rich."

"I just want to be with you."

"Let's take it one day at a time and see if you still feel that way in a month from now."

"Sounds like a plan."

They exchanged phone numbers and then made passionate love one more time. After they dressed, Marvin kissed Cindy and said good-bye.

"Thanks for everything, I'll be watching you on the six o'clock news tonight. I'm your biggest fan!"

"You'd better be," she noticed his erection and laughed. "I'll call you after my broadcast. There's always a lot to do to get ready for the show."

"Ok, I love you."

Marvin left the penthouse and drove home.

CHAPTER FIFTEEN

Back to Brooklyn

Marvin parked his unmarked police car in front of his house just behind a bus stop. As he walked to his apartment door, he couldn't stop thinking about Cindy and what happened to him in the last few days.

He walked in and found his mother waiting.

"Are you crazy?" she demanded. "Where have you been for the last three days? Your father would turn over in his grave if he knew you became a cop. The phone's been ringing off the hook. I have the mayor's office calling for you, a man named Big Mo called a dozen times and said it's an emergency, Steve Sender called and said the same thing, and a woman from San Francisco named Betty called to say she's worried about you and offered to come to New York if you need her for anything. The news anchor Cindy Sears from NBC called to say she misses you and loves you and will call after seven tonight.

"Some gay police organization called GOAL called and asked to speak to the president, named Super Jew. To top it all off, Truman Capote called and said you won. He will fund the gay organization and you and your boyfriends are invited to his black-and-white ball at the Plaza Hotel. There are plenty of other phone messages too I've got pages of them."

"Mom, I'm tired," he said. "I'll deal with the messages later. I need some sleep."

The phone rang.

"Whoever it is, tell them I'm not home," he said.

Edith answered and it is Mayor John Lindsay on the phone. She turned to Marvin and whispered who it is on the phone.

"I'll call him back, "Marvin whispered back. "I'm not home."

Edith gave the message and hung up. "Marvin, you sure have changed in a week."

"I have to get some sleep; I had a rough night. When I get up, we'll have a long talk. I have a story you won't believe. Just one thing: if Cindy Sears calls wake me up. I want to talk to her. She's the only one I want to talk too."

....

Six hours later, Edith tried to wake him from a sound sleep, "Marvin? Marvin! Wake up. It's Cindy on the phone."

He tried to get up but realized he had an erection and was embarrassed to let his mother see it. "Tell her to call back in ten minutes. I'm having a hard time waking up." He smiled.

Edith came back a minute later. "She said she'd come to our house pick you up at eight in her car. Dinner is her treat."

"Tell Cindy it's a date. What time is it?"

"It's four o'clock."

"Great. I can sleep for another hour."

He fell asleep again.

....

Edith woke him at five o'clock. After Marvin had a cup of coffee, he started returning the calls. First, he called Mayor John Lindsay and was surprised to see that the number he left was his private line.

"Hello?"

"Hi, Mayor Lindsay. It's Super Jew. I'm returning your call."

"I'm glad you did. I want to tell you that the City of New York will do whatever you need to get GOAL off the ground. The other thing is I want you to contact Truman Capote and get me and my five friends invited to the black-and white ball.""That will not be a problem for the invite to the black and white ball for you and your party."

"Thanks," Mayor said, "Super Jew. I promise you a promotion to first-grade detective as soon as you're off probation. By the way, I heard through the grapevine that you're going out with Governor Nelson Rockefellers' niece, Cindy. Is that true?"

"Wow. There are no secrets in this city. It is true. I'm an incredibly lucky guy."

"I'll see you at the ball. We can talk about your future in the police department. Maybe you could join my administration. Remember you must act gay in public. Don't blow it."

"We'll talk. See you at the ball." He hung up.

"What did he say?" Edith asked.

"He offered me a job in his administration and promised my promotion to first-grade detective. Mom, I must check the bottom of my shoes. I must have stepped in some shit because that's how lucky I've been."

"I'll leave you alone to return more of those calls."

"Thanks, Mom. I love you."

He started down the list. All the callers had the same theme. Marvin was becoming a star and a hero in the city. All the movers and shakers wanted to help him any way they could.

He saved Truman Capote's call for last. He couldn't wait to speak to him. "Mom, pick up the extension and unscrew the bottom part, so Truman won't be able to hear you."

Marvin called, and Truman answered quickly.

"Hello?"

"How does it feel to lose a bet, Truman?"

"Is that you, Super Jew?"

"Yes."

"How does it feel to be a gay policeman in the city?"

"Since I've been gay, I never got laid so much in my life. In fact, I'm going out with a Rockefeller."

"Who? Nelson?"

"No, his niece, Elizabeth. Boy, is she pretty, and we really hit it off. I'm in love with her."

"I know her. She is the anchor on NBC News. You're right, she's beautiful, but you can't take her to the black-and white ball as your date, because you'd blow the whole thing about being gay. You must take a male with you. If the press finds out you're not gay, we will not be able to start GOAL, and a lot of people are counting on GOAL being able to serve the gay community."

Marvin thought for a second. "I have an idea. Why don't we have Cindy sit at Mayor Lindsay's table?" "I hate that guy, Mayor Lindsay! He's never done shit to help the gay community."

"I spoke to the Mayor. He's giving GOAL his total support and asked me to call him if we need anything. He couldn't have been nicer. I'm asking this as a favor. Please invite the mayor and his five friends to the ball, and let Cindy sit with them."

"Only if I get to pick your date. You have to dance with him, too."

"You've got me by the balls. OK. It's a deal."

"If anything comes up, I'll get in touch." Truman hung up.

Edith put the extension phone back together and ran from the bedroom. "If I hadn't heard what he said on the phone, I never would be able to believe what you're going to tell me."

"Mom, what I'm about to say has to be top secret. Promise me."

"I promise."

He trusted her, knowing she was always on his side. She's been a straight shooter all her life, giving Marvin the best advice.

He explained everything that happened from his arrest on the train to falling in love with Cindy.

"Marvin, most mothers would tell their son to confess and stop living a lie, but if you do, the city and police department will come down on you like a ton of bricks.

"your father always told you do the best thing for yourself as long as you didn't hurt anyone. Keep up the lie. You have my total support. I'll back you. In the long run, it'll work out for you and the police department, and you'll make a better life for yourself and Cindy."

"Thanks, Mom. I knew you'd give me the right advice. I love you and I miss Dad."

I bet Dad is smiling up in heaven. When he's looking down on us and he find out that I'm acting gay and I'm the first president of GOAL, Dad must be laughing in his ass off.

But this a I promise you and Dad I won't hurt anyone with lies."

"You would make Dad proud of what you are doing for civil rights. Bye the way I can't wait to meet Cindy." Edith said, excited.

Cindy Comes to Brooklyn

When Cindy arrived at Marvin's apartment on Ocean Parkway and rang the bell, Edith opened the door to greet her.

"Marvin told me he met a beautiful, smart woman and he was right. I watch you all the time on TV."

"You must be his mother. Thank you for the compliment."

They hugged.

Marvin came to the front door and kissed Cindy before inviting her inside.

"I'm starved," she said. "I haven't eaten since lunch. Where would like to have dinner? It's my treat."

"How about Nathan's? It's in Coney Island."

"I've never been there. What kind of cuisine is it?"

"I guess American." He laughed.

Cindy knew he was playing a joke on her. She also knew Nathan's was famous for its hot dogs.

"Maybe after dinner, we'll enjoy some rides and have a fun night on Coney Island."

"I love roller coasters," she said, "and amusement rides."

"Great. Let's go."

They said good-bye to Edith and drove to Coney Island, which was only ten minutes from Marvin's house. They parked Cindy's Ford Mustang on Stillwell Avenue and Surf, where mounted New York officers were on duty. Marvin identified himself as a detective, so the officers allowed him to park. After thanking them, Marvin and Cindy left.

Nathan's was begun by a Polish immigrant named Nathan Handwerker in 1916 with a $300 loan from friends. He sold his famous hot dogs for five cent and soon became a big hit. It didn't take him long to sell over a million hot dogs on Coney Island.

As they approached Nathan's, Cindy stopped and looked at the place." I never had dinner here before. This will a first for me."

"I'll bet you'll love the hot dogs and French fries."

"It smells delicious."

"I'll get in line to place our orders. You can get our drinks in the other line. I'll have a grape soda will meet you at the table facing Surf Avenue.

"There are no chairs! We have to stand up to eat?"

"It's traditional to eat hot dogs standing up. The good news is that the hot dogs cost fifteen cents each and their fries won't break the bank either, as they cost the same. They taste great too.

Marvin waited in line, got their food, and met Cindy at a table carrying four hot dogs and two large bags of French fries. She had two large grape sodas in large plastic cups.

"How do you like your hot dogs, with mustard or relish?" Marvin asked.

"Mustard."

"Same here." He went to a table where a large bowl of mustard sat. The taste of Nathan's mustard was the best in the world.

Marvin returned to their table. Cindy took one bite of her hot dog and said, "These tastes better than the Four Seasons!"

"I knew you'd love this."

"I have to ask you something. I told some of my fellow reporters at the station that I'm going out with you, and they all said you're gay. But you absolutely don't act gay? Is that true that you are gay? Super Jew?"

In a confident, reassuring voice, Marvin said, "Let me lay my cards on the table. I'm not gay." He explained what Truman Capote did.

"He pulled a trick on me and spread the rumor I'm gay, but the good news is he put me in a position to give all gay police officers their civil rights by asking me to be president of GOAL.

I won the bet with Turman. When I announced at the press conference that Truman Capote will fund GOAL from his own pocket. I put him into a position where he couldn't refuse to fund GOAL.

"I already won the game of being gay. I really believe I can help my fellow officers who happen to be gay to get their civil rights. It is a win-win situation. Anyone who knows me will know I'm not gay. And if someone thinks I'm gay, I don't give a shit if they think gay or not."

"Super Jew, you'll change the police department's attitude towards gays for the better. I'm proud of you. You can count on me for support."

"Thanks. I'll need it. Now give me a kiss to make sure I'm not gay."

She grabbed him and gave him the biggest kiss of his life.

After they finished eating, he asked, "Let's go on some rides."

"Sounds like fun."

The Cyclone opened on June 25, 1927. It was a historic roller coaster that was 2,640 feet long with an eighty-five-foot drop to give riders the thrill of their lives.

Cindy and Marvin went to the ticket booth to buy tickets, which cost fifty cents each.

"That's more than I paid for dinner.

Cindy laughed. "Don't worry about the price. I'm a Rockefeller."

As they walked up the platform, he said, "Let's get in the front car. You can see where you're going."

They got into the front car of the Cyclone, and the attendant closed the metal bar tightly against their stomach.

Cindy turned toward Marvin. "I've never been on a roller coaster in my life."

"You picked the toughest one in the world to ride. I'll make sure nothing bad happens to you."

He put his arm around her and held her close to keep her safe.

It was an amazing ride. The first big drop was eighty-five feet. They went from zero to sixty miles an hour in about ten seconds. A sharp left turn almost crushed Marvin against the side of the car. Cindy screamed at the top of her lungs. Their bodies vibrated with the shaking.

After all the drops, turns, abrupt accelerations and sudden stops, the car came to a final halt back at the platform. Marvin and Cindy stood to get out but had trouble with their balance. They helped each other out.

"That was some ride," Cindy said. "What does my hair look like?"

"Your hair's a mess. Let's go to the boardwalk and find a bathroom where you can fix it. Then we can walk back to the car. We'll hold hands and look at the ocean and full moon. Who knows? We might fall in love. We'll see if you want to try any more rides after that."

"I'm already in love with you, Super Jew. I love rides, but what would you like to do?"

"I like to dance. How about we drive to Bay Ridge and visit some of the great clubs like Pastels, Mustard Seed, or the Brown Derby. You choose."

"I've heard that Pastels is a hip place. Let's see if we can get in. There's usually a line around the block to get in there."

"I have an in. The security guards are off-duty cops."

"Then let's do some dancing."

Bay Ridge, Brooklyn—Pastels Go-Go Club

Marvin and Cindy pulled up to the front of Pastels and parked the police car. They saw a line snaking around the block.

Two big off-duty cops that work as security guards and the manager approached their car. The manager looked in and smiled.

"Hey, Super Jew, can I help you?" he asked.

"I've got Cindy Spears from NBC News with me. I was telling her that Pastels is the in-spot in Brooklyn to party. Can you get us in without waiting in line?

"is the Pope Catholic? Just park a little way from the entrance, and we'll keep an eye on your car."

Marvin and Cindy were escorted into the disco club past the long line of people still waiting. As they passed the round bar, ten deep with partiers waiting to order drinks, they saw that the typical man wore red pants with a black stripe, bell-bottom pants, and platform shoes with three-inch heels, a large black belt, and a psychedelic shirt with an open collar to allow his chest hair to show.

The women wore noticeably short miniskirts with large belts, long white boots to their thighs, and psychedelic blouses.

Marvin and Cindy fit right in. As they walked around the disco, they smelled the strong scent of marijuana. Marvin saw many of the couples on the chairs toward the back of the club smoking joints and passing them around.

"Do you want to get out of here?" Cindy asked. "I don't want you to feel embarrassed by all the marijuana in here."

"I'm off duty. I don't give a dam what they do. Do you want to dance?"

"Sure."

They walked onto the dance floor, where psychedelic lights spun around the club so brightly, they almost blinded people. Two large cages on the side of the stage held two go-go dancers.

Marvin and Cindy did the jerk with all the other dancers on the floor. They danced until four o'clock the next morning with only an occasional break. When the club finally played the last song and the lights came on, it seemed like no one had left yet. The place was still packed.

Marvin gave Cindy a long, hard kiss. "I think we should make like a tree and leave."

They walked out holding hands.

Marvin thanked the guards for keeping watch on his car.

"Super Jew, we're cops from the Ninety-ninth Precinct. We'll see you when you come in," one guard said.

"I'll buy you guys a drink the next time I see you," Marvin replied. "Thanks for everything."

Cindy and Marvin got into the police car, and then she tuned to him.

"I had a great time with you today," she said. "I'm in love with you. I hope you're in love with me, too."

"Cindy, this is our first date, but I know I'm in love with you. I think I might be rushing things, but would it be too soon to ask you to marry me?"

"Wow!" she exclaimed, surprised. "That is a first, a proposal on the first date. We can't go to your apartment. How about you stay at my place?" "I'd be delighted to stay with you, but my mother might stop talking me if I don't call her and tell her not to worry."

Marvin went back into the club to use their phone to call home. When he got back to the car, he told Cindy, "She started screaming at the top of her lungs. She's right. It's four in the morning, I didn't realize the time. Time certainly goes fast when you're having fun. Let's go. I have three hours until I have to be at work."

"Maybe you should sleep in Brooklyn tonight. You'd save thirty minutes on your drive to work."

"I have to drive you home, anyway. If I leave you. I won't be sleeping thinking about you all night."

"What time do you have to leave for work?"

"I have to be on the road by seven."

They drove to Cindy's condo.

• • • • • • • • • • •

Once they were in bed, they fell sound asleep in moments. Marvin was still fully dressed. Cindy tried to rouse him without success.

She removed his clothes, hoping to make him more comfortable, but he never woke up. She hoped he wasn't dead. When she saw him still breathing, she was relieved?

Cindy undressed and got into bed, putting her arms around him. She couldn't sleep. She kissed Marvin's forehead and rubbed against him.

Half-asleep, he woke and smiled at her. "I thought all the angels were in heaven. I must be dreaming." He was asleep again in seconds.

Cindy set her alarm for six-fifteen and went to sleep, too.

• • • • • • • • • • •

When the alarm went off, both woke up. Marvin had an erection, which Cindy felt when she hugged him. "Is that a gun in your underwear, or are glad to see me?"

Marvin laughed. "I'm very happy to see you."

Cindy kissed him. He returned the kiss, and a few seconds later, they were making passionate love.

Once they finished, Marvin looked at the clock and saw it was 6:50. "I have to get to work." He put on his uniform, socks, and shoes like a fireman responding to a fire.

He finished dressing and brushed his teeth in four minutes. He kissed Cindy at the door and said, "I'll call when I can. I love you."

"Be safe, Super Jew. I love you."

Marvin got in his unmarked car and put on the lights and siren, as he drove down the New York streets as fast as he could. He went through red lights and zoomed through traffic until he pulled up at the Twenty-first Precinct, where he was supposed to report in for 7:45 roll call in the muster room.

CHAPTER SIXTEEN

The Twenty-first Precinct

Marvin parker his unmarked car in the precinct's parking lot and walked inside. He approached the desk where Lieutenant Paddy O'Shea, the desk officer in charge of the precinct, gave him a look that could kill. He put his right hand on his reading glasses and adjusted them to the tip of his nose to get a better look at Marvin.

"Are you detective Super Jew?"

"Yes, Lieutenant."

O'Shea's face broke into a warm smile. "Detective, the precinct captain's been expecting you."

He gave Marvin a piece of paper and told him to fill out his tax registry number and detective shield number so the information could be entered into the official police blotter.

"Detective Super Jew, your locker number is 1972. You'll need to get a padlock for it. You're assigned to the Twenty-first Precinct's detective squad. After you see the captain, you'll go to the detective squad room and meet the commanding officer of your squad.

"The first thing we'll get you is a dress suit, so you look the part. We have a couple of clothing stores that will furnish you with a suit. You can throw away that rookie uniform. They'll tell you your assignment and what is expected of you to do as detective."

Marvin stared at Lieutenant O'Shea in amazement. "Lieutenant, I don't have that much money on me to buy a suit."

"Son don't worry about the cost. It's on the arm. You'll find out that you don't dip into your pocket for most things. They're part of the benefit of being a detective. This a job where you go home with more money than you brought to work."

"Thanks, Lieutenant."

"You're dismissed. You should go up to meet Captain Sammy Katz, our commanding officer."

Marvin went up the stairs until he reached the proper floor and walked down the hall. At the captain's door, he knocked.

"Come in," Captain Katz said.

Marvin entered the office and looked around. The walls were filled with pictures of cats—lions, leopards, and even house cats. On the captain's desk stood brass statues of cats in different positions.

I think the captain's nuts. Marvin thought.

Captain Katz stood up from behind his desk and shook Marvin's hand. "I'm glad to have you in the Twenty-first Precinct. From one Jewish policeman to another, anything you need. I'm here for you. I know you're the president of GOAL, and I have orders from the commissioner to do anything I can to assist you in getting that organization started. Mayor Lindsay's office called, too, with the same offer.

"I got a strange call from Governor Nelson Rockefeller's office. They want you to call him on his direct line. What's that about?"

"Captain, it' a long story. I'm close friends with his niece. The governor wants to make sure I have no trouble in the department because I'm gay."

"Super Jew, I never met anyone in the police force with that many hooks. I promise you nobody in the Twenty-first Precinct will give you any difficulty. Come to me first if anyone gives you any grief. I promise to straighten it out. You must promise me you'll come to me with any complaints, so I can work it out in house.

"I promise I'll see you first, Captain."

"Go ahead and call the governor use my phone. I'll leave and close door, so your conversation will be private."

"Thanks, Captain. I'll make that call now."

Captain Katz left his office and closed the door behind him. He went to the detective squad room and into Lieutenant Detective Dick Mason's the commanding officers of the detective squard.

"I want to listen in to Super Jew's conversation with the governor," he said.

Mason called the switchboard operator and told her to tap Captain Katz's phone so they could listen to a conversation. The call was already in progress when they broke in, but the only thing they missed were the greetings the two men exchanged.

"Super Jew, I had a long talk with Cindy about you," Governor Rockefeller said. "After what she said, I'm extremely impressed. I plan to run for president in four years. If I could count on you and GOAL for your support with the gay community, that would really help my presidential campaign."

"Governor, I promise you our full support for president or if you run for New York state governor again."

"Thanks, I'm counting on you. Cindy told me a lot about you. You know she's in love with you. We're very proud of her and what she's accomplished in life. I want to welcome you into the Rockefeller family. Since you're part of the family now, any time we can do something for you, all you have to do is ask."

"Thank you, Governor."

"I have a lot of influence with the mayor of New York, and the police commissioner owes me many favors. Whatever you need, I can help you in the police department. If anyone gives you a hard time, I promise to take care of him."

Captain Katz covered the mouthpiece with his hand and looked at Lieutenant Mason. "Holy shit. We're screwed. We will all go to jail if Super Jew finds out about the police pad. Can we cut him in on the gambling money coming in each month? We are counting on that money for ourselves just to pay our bills.

"Captain, someone will have to approach Super Jew and see if he wants in first. I'll have the precinct bagman take him on a run to pick up money and see how he reacts."

"That is a big gamble, the captain said nervously. "If he turns us in, we're all going to jail.

"What other option do we have? There's no way to hide the pad. It's an open secret in the precinct."

"I won't be able to sleep tonight because I'll be worrying how Super Jew will react to the pad. We have to make him happy and give him anything he wants."

"I couldn't agree more, the Captain said."

· · · · · · · · · · ·

Marvin thanked the governor for his offer of help, then he hung up. He waited in the office for the captain to return, which he did within five minutes.

"Did everything go well with Governor Rockefeller?"

"Captain, you may not believe me, but he said he can't do enough for me. If anyone in the city gives me a hard time, the governor said he'd handle it."

"That's unbelievable. I promise we'll take care of you in any way we can. Whenever you need a day off, just ask. I'll make sure we don't charge you for any vacation days while you're off.

"Now for the good news. After you make your first arrest, I'll promote you to detective second grade, with a raise that'll make your pay equal to a sergeant. All you must do is play ball and not make any waves. Got it?"

"What kind of arrest do I need to make?"

"Don't worry. We'll assign you to, let's say, a murder arrest, and we'll give you the credit for the investigation, too. I'm an expert when it comes to writing promotion forms.

"One other thing—we have a pad in the Twenty-first precinct that we split by ranks. I get a full share as captain Lieutenants get three-quarter shares, sergeants get a half share, and detectives get a quarter share. That is the same as the New York City pay scale."

"Take it from an old-timer. You must treat people you meet except your partner like mushrooms. Keep them in the dark and feed them shit. Always have a story ready to cover your ass. If you want to keep a secret, never tell anyone. If you tell even one person, it's not a secret anymore. What I just told you is more than you'll would ever learn in the Police Academy. You are in the real world, now."

"Just one question, Captain. What's a pad?"

"Wow. A pad is the money we pick up from gambling locations within the precinct. Nobody gives a dam about gambling, so the money is considered clean. We have a gentleman's agreement with gamblers in our precinct. We help them, and they help us solve crimes with inside information.

"You'll soon find out that most crimes our detectives solve come from information from other people—the mailman, the utility workers, and the gamblers. We get direct information from them, and one hand always washes the other. We take good care of our informers."

"You have my word I won't see anything that goes on in the precinct. I promise to keep my mouth shut."

"If anyone from the Twenty-first Precinct shook down and took money from a drug dealer, we'd lock up that cop for good. There's clean money and dirty money. You have to know the difference."

"I'll send you out with Detective Rocky Scale, our precinct bagman. He'll introduce you to people who can help you solve crimes in our precinct. He'll also get you a couple of suits, ties, and a trench coat. Remember to get the diamond and gold pinky ring. That's part of being a detective. It goes with the job."

Marvin thought that over and nodded. "Captain, you can count on me. What will be my share once I'm promoted to second-grade detective?"

"Off the top of my head, I think it's around $500 a month."

"That's twice what I'm making!"

"You just got a hundred-percent raise."

They laughed. Captain Katz called the desk officer and asked for Detective Rocky Scala to be sent to his office immediately.

Detective Scala quickly entered the office and stood before the captain's desk to at attention and saluted.

"At ease, Rocky," the captain said. "I'd like you to meet our new detective, Super Jew. I want you to show him around the precinct and introduce him to the movers and shakers here. I also want you to pick up the monthly pad with him"

"Can you vouch for him, Captain? I heard he's gay and is in with the governor and mayor."

"See, Super Jew?" the captain asked. "If you tell even one person, it's not a secret anymore. Rocky you found out about Super Jew in a hurry. I'll vouch for him."

"It's your call, Captain." He walked over to Super Jew and shook his hand. "Welcome aboard, Super Jew. You're part of the team."

"I'll leave you two alone, so Rocky can give you the ground rules on what's expected from you." Captain Katz left the office.

"You're already made a name for yourself, Super Jew," Rocky said. "How long have you been on the job?"

"This is the start of my second week."

"You've got less than two weeks on the force, and you're up for second-grade detective? Holy shit! I've been on the job for nineteen years, and I'm a third-grade detective who has to kiss ass just to keep my job!"

"Nobody said life was fair," Marvin joked, making both them laugh.

"I'll take you under my wing and show you the ropes. Let's start with the rules. First, don't tell anyone about what you do on the job. Second, never tell anybody about the pad you'll get every month, especially your wife or girlfriend. If you break up or get divorced, your loved one will have the money you received on the pad to hang you in court. That won't go well with any of us because that will cause a big internal investigation and cops will go to jail. Got it?"

"Look Super Jew its not that we want to take money from gamblers. It's that a cop pay is very low and its almost impossible to live on with a family with what the city pays us."

"Here's an example. We had a detective's Christmas party with all the detectives from the precinct and their families. At the table, one of the wives brought up the fact that her husband got an extra $800 cash for Christmas. The other detectives' wives wanted to know where he got the money! That dumb bitch caused a lot of problems, and some of the detectives ended up divorced soon after."

"Wow, there's a lot to learn about this job. When do I receive my first pad payment?"

"I like how you think. I love doing business with Jews. There's no bullshit. It's all about the money."

They both smiled.

"There's more to learn, but you'll understand when we go out to pick up the envelopes. Before I forget, when and if you're transferred or lose your job, you stay on the pad for six months after you leave.

"You'll start getting pad money on May third. It looks like you'll get about $600 a month, which will go up to $800 when you're promoted to second grade. The pad pays on the third of each month, just like Social Security."

"Gee, I never thought I'd start getting Social Security at the ripe old age of twenty-one!" Marvin exclaimed.

"Don't flaunt your newfound wealth. That's the fastest way to get into trouble. You can't go out and buy new car, a big house, fancy jewelry or new watches. You need a good place to store your money. I'd tell you what mine hiding place is, but then it wouldn't be a secret anymore. Everyone should have such a problem, where to hide extra money!" Rocky explained.

"I'm starting to love police work even more." replied Marvin.

"Let's go out on the street and meet our clients, the gamblers who pay our bills. One other thing. They'll mention a guy named Big Mo. He's the top dog in the gambling organization in the entire city. I've never met him, but that guy has all the power in the city, so don't joke about him. He can get you fired." added Rocky.

I know Big Mo Dash, Marvin thought. *Am I really that lucky?*

"First, let's get you a good suit, a trench coats and shoes. Then we'll do our rounds." said Rocky.

They left the office, went to their unmarked police car, and drove from the lot, stopping in front of Sydney Fine's customized tailored clothing shop. Rocky and Marvin walked in, and Sydney greeted them.

"You're two days late, Rocky," Sydney said. "I couldn've given you information on that bank robbery. They broke into the bank at nine o'clock in the evening, punched a hole into the vault, and emptied the whole bank vault into a stolen moving van. It happened last night near the Brooklyn Bridge. The robbers tied up the security guard and ended up shooting and killing him."

"Even with that information, Sydney," Rocky said, "We can't arrest people before they commit a crime. Let me introduce you to our new detective. Super Jew, I'm showing him the ropes."

"I saw you on the news," Sydney told Marvin. "A Jewish detective, man you have a good future in the police department."

"Thanks, Sydney."

"Here's your monthly pad from the boys, Rocky." He handed Rocky an envelope stuffed with cash.

Rocky took the large envelope without looking opening the envelope and counting the cash and slid it into a coat pocket. "Thanks. Now that we've got that out of the way, who are the, mutts who committed the robbery?" asked Rocky.

Sydney handed Rocky a piece of paper with some names on it. "I hope to hell you catch those animals. With all the riots, looting and chaos going on right now, the officers are tied up protecting each other and have no time to patrol the city. Those robbers knew they had plenty of time to break into the vault and loot it. It gave them the perfect opportunity to commit their crime and get away."

Rocky studied the names. "We know these guys and where they live. Super Jew, do you want the collar for a bank robbery?"

"Is it really this easy to make an arrest?" Marvin asked.

"No, sometimes, it's easier," replied Rocky.

"Sure, I'd love this arrest." Marvin smiled.

"Use police jargon, it's a collar." Rocky turned to Sydney, "I need to ask a favor, Super Jew needs a couple of suits. What can you do for him?"

"It would be an honor to have him wear my suits. I'll take some measurements now. He can have the suits in two days."

"How much will they cost?" Marvin asked.

"Nothing," answered Sydney. "But when I call you, I want you coming to my shop when I close and take me to the bank in your police car to make a cash deposit."

"It would be my pleasure to give you a ride to the bank."

"I like you, Super Jew."

After the measurements, Rocky and Marvin returned to their police car.

"I have to ask you something, Rocky. Is this the pad Captain Katz mentioned? How come you didn't count the money?"

"We never count it. That would be rude. Sydney collects the money and information for the detective from all the gamblers in the Twenty-first Precinct. We don't have to come into contact with the gamblers directly. We stop at Sydney's once a week."

"You'll be taking him to the bank. That means you're in charge of picking up the pad and information from him. That frees me up to do other things you don't want to know about."

"Looks like I got promoted to bagman."

"You're right, Super Jew, and that pays a lot more than the police department jobs. Let's go make some bank robber collars."

They drove to Leroy Brown, a street hustler, who made a nice living working the streets of the Twenty-first Precinct. Leroy bought liquor on Saturday when the liquor store was open. Then due to the blue laws, the liquor stores were closed on Sundays, so Leroy sold his liquor each Sunday for a nice profit. He also washed the luxury cars for the pimps and drug dealers using free water from the fire hydrants on the streets. He knew everything about illegal activities in the precinct.

Rocky and Marvin pulled up and saw Leroy washing a new, long white brand-new Cadillac with gold continental wheels on the rear bumper. The car is the definition of a pimp mobile.

Leroy walked to the driver's door and shook Rocky's hand. "What's up, Rocky? I see you have Super Jew as a partner. Talk on the street is that he's going to try to make a name for himself on the job."

"That's bullshit," Rocky said. "He's one of us, and I promise we can work together."

"Leroy, I'm here to help you help me," Marvin said. "You work with me, and I'll work with you. Let's start with where we can find these three assholes?"

Rocky took a piece of paper and a pen and asked Leroy, "What are the names and addresses of the three bank robbers?"

Leroy gave him the information, and it matched what Sydney had given them.

"They're holed up in Fiftieth Navy Street in a building near the Brooklyn Navy Yard. Those idiots blabbed about the job before they did it. It wasn't hard to figure out who heisted that bank."

"Word on the street is that they hatched the plan when they saw all the riots in the city. They felt the timing was perfect, so they wouldn't get caught. They bragged about it to me and their friends, how they would get into the vault and steal a pickup truck to use. I told them they were nuts. With all the money they were about to steal, they'd be killed buy the mob always wants their cut of the take. "They said they could take care of the mob! They wanted to start a new black gang with the money they took. They said it was time to start a black gang to take business away from the mob."

"Everybody's after them. They hit it big time. I heard they got hundreds of grand from the bank. You'd be doing us a favor if you arrested them. They put a lot of heat on our community from the mob. If they're found before you get there, they'll be robbed and killed, and they know it."

"I've been to that place many times. They're on the third floor on Fiftieth Navy Street."

"Thanks Leroy," Rocky said. "We owe you one."

"Thanks a lot," Marvin said. "It was nice meeting you. I owe you one too. In fact, you're invited to my next Bar Mitzvah."

Leroy laughed. "I'll be there with my ham sandwich."

All three men laughed.

Rocky and Marvin drove toward Fiftieth Navy Street.

"This is some serious hit, Super Jew," Rocky said. We could call for backup to raid the place, or we could risk trying to collar them ourselves. If we do it, there'll be a big reward in it for us."

"You mean we'd make a great arrest and be in all the newspapers?"

"No, you idiot. We get to keep part of the loot. It's your call."

"Rocky, I never did anything like this before," Marvin said nervously. "I don't know if I could sleep at night if we steal the stolen loot."

"With the money you're getting, you won't be sleeping alone. You can have all the women you want. Don't be a schmuck. This is an opportunity to have a great future and live the good life."

"What the hell," Marvin said, feeling excited. "Count me in!"

"Just one thing, never tell anyone about this and don't start spending money like a drunken sailor, ok?"

"I promise."

"I know this building. It's full of drug addicts and homeless people. I want you to climb to the roof and come down the fire escape. Look into their bedroom window with your gun drawn. If those three idiots try anything, you must shoot them before they shoot me through the front door. Got it? I'll come to the front door and ask them to surrender. You'll be able to hear me from the fire escape. I'll be able to hear you at the front door, just shout when you give commands to the skels."

Fiftieth Navy Street

Rocky and Marvin arrived at Fiftieth Navy Street in their unmarked police car, though a blind man could see they were cops. A large crowd of drug addicts sat on the corner, but they ran off, scattering hypodermic needles and drug paraphernalia as they ran. Rocky and Marvin parked around the corner away from the building's entrance.

The two men got out and walked back toward the entrance. After agreeing on their plans, they set their watches. Rocky would enter the apartment at ten minutes after the hour.

They climbed four flights of stairs to the apartment they wanted, then Marvin went to the roof and climbed down the fire escape to the correct window He drew his new service revolver and cocked it, and he peered through the window to see a robber at a desk with a stack of manila envelopes in front of him. He was writing on one envelope while his two buddies sat around the bed with a pile of cash, gold, and diamond jewelry, trying to divide the take three ways. Cash and jewelry took up most of the bed in a pile almost three feet high.

Against the far wall, Marvin saw open safety-deposit boxes stacked to the ceiling. He counted over forty of them and there had to be hundreds of safety-deposit boxes sack in rows that took up most of the three walls of the bedroom. Two guns lay on the front of the bed near the cash and jewelry.

They definitely got into the vault and clean-out and the bank vault and stole those safety-deposit boxes. Marvin thought. *There must be millions of dollars on the bed!*

Glancing at his wristwatch, he saw he had two minutes before Rocky would enter the room. Marvin felt excited and strangely immune to harm, as if nothing could go wrong. He stepped away from the window and waited. Two minutes felt like an eternity.

When the time came, Marvin squatted closer to the window for cover and aimed at the three men. "Hands up!" he shouted. "This is the police! They have two guns." he added for Rocky's benefit.

"Make them kick the guns to you," Rocky shouted back.

"Pick up the guns with you left hands," Marvin told the men. "Put them on the floor and kick them to the window." He stood at the fire escape keeping his gun aimed at them.

One of the robbers began crying, pleading with Super Jew not to shoot them. The other two didn't move and stared at Marvin. The crying man picked up a gun with his left and hand and kicked it to the window where Marvin stood.

Marvin bent down and reached through the open window with his right hand, his gun he put in his left hand, so he could to pick up the robber's gun. His eyes remained on the three men. Before Marvin could blink, one of the two men grabbed the remaining gun from the bed and fired at Marvin.

Without thinking Marvin emptied the gun he just picked up with his right hand, also firing rapidly with his left. He hit all three men in their heads and chests. They were dead before they hit the floor. All six shots from the robber gun missed and went into the ceiling over Marvin's head.

Marvin couldn't believe he hadn't been hit. He was so excited, he climbed in through the window and began kicking the robber's heads. He took the gun from the man who tried to shoot him.

He realized Rocky was screaming, "let me in," at him from the front door and Marvin rush over to the door to let him in. Rocky ran in to the apartment.

"Super Jew, are you OK?"

"Yeah, I think so."

Rocky saw the money on the bed. "The hell with these guys! Start filling pillowcases with money."

"What about calling an ambulance?"

Rocky saw the bloody head wounds. "These idiots are dead as doornails. We'll take care of them after we take care of us. First, get as many pillowcases as you can and fill them with money from the bed. Leave of the money as evidence. I'll get our car and park it by the mailbox in front of the building. You bring the pillowcases down as fast as you can."

"Rocky, can you make sure I wasn't shot?" Marvin asked.

Rocky gave him a quick once over. "Turn around. There's no blood on you. They missed. Look over that window frame. I see at least four shots in the wall. What bad shots those guys were. "

"Thank God!" replied Marvin.

"Enough talk," Rocky said sternly. "I'll get the car and meet you downstairs with the money."

"Should I count what I put into the pillowcases?"

"No, just fill them as fast as you can try not to step in any blood. Remember, this is a crime scene."

"Somebody must've heard all those shots. They'll call for help."

"In this neighborhood, with all the riots going on, nobody sees or hears anything. They never call the cops. If they do, you just thank the cops for coming and tell them we collared three bank robbers."

Rocky ran out the door, while Marvin stepped over the blood on the floor and began filling the pillowcases as fast as he could. When he finished, he stepped back over the bodies with king-sized pillowcases filled with cash.

He dragged them down four flights of stairs and used one of them to prop the front door open. Rocky waited by the big mailbox on Navy Street. He grabbed four of the pillowcases and helped Marvin toss them into the trunk of the police car.

"There are more upstairs," Marvin said.

They made two trips to carry down as much cash as they could. Soon, the police car was so full of pillowcases stuff full of cash, they couldn't add any more. The front and back seats of the police car were so full of king size pillowcases of cash, they couldn't see out the rear and passenger side window.

"I'll be back as fast as I can after I hide these," Rocky said. "It'll take me about thirty minutes. Don't do anything, just stay in the apartment and don't touch anything."

"You want me to stay in the apartment with three dead people? I can't do that!"

"I don't have time for this, Super Jew!" It's only thirty minutes. This will change your life. You'll be rich!"

"Ok, come back as soon as you can. I don't like being with corpses." Rocky sped off.

Marvin turned around, bumping into the large mailbox, and returned to the apartment with its dead bodies and piles of jewelry and cash on the bed. As he climbed the stairs, he wondered, *Can I trust Rocky? He didn't give a shit if I was shot or not. Where will he hide the money? How much did we get? He might try to cheat me.*

Marvin investigated the apartment and saw the bodies were already turning purple, and they didn't smell too good. He went to the desk and saw postage stamps. It seemed one robber planned to mail the cash and jewelry to his wife in manila envelopes.

What a great idea. Why don't I do that? He could fill the envelopes and mail cash and jewelry to himself from the mailbox downstairs. He had thirty minutes before Rocky would return.

He started writing out envelopes with the return address of *Santa Claus, 100 Easy Street, North Pole, New York, 10001.* He attached ten eight-cent stamps to the envelopes and began filling them with cash and jewelry. Soon, he had nineteen full envelopes. He dumped them into the mailbox and made sure none of them got stuck going down.

When he returned to the apartment, he hadn't been there more than a minute before Rocky returned.

Rocky came in and saw Marvin sweating profusely. "I know you're shitting your pants. Here's our story!"

Rocky explained that they had a tip from an informer and went to investigate. They planned to call for backup if they needed to do a raid, but as they stopped the car one of the robbers saw them and ran into the building. Rocky and Marvin chase the one robber and went to the roof, then Super Jew followed the robber down the fire escape. Rocky went downstairs to cover the front door. Before Rocky could get to the front door of the apartment, he heard gunshots and that when I called a 10-13 for backup.

"Got it," Marvin said. "That should work. I have a few questions. How much money do you think we got? Where'd you hide the loot, just in case something happens to you."

"Super Jew," Rocky said skeptically, "don't you trust me?"

"Money is money!" Marvin smirked.

"I don't have a clue how much it is. The pillowcases are in my basement in the laundry room. Some of them are in the clothes dryer. After we get interviewed and are off duty, we'll go to my house and count it. Then we can split all the loot. The only problem is, I have company sleeping at my house, so we must be discreet.

"Rocky, thanks for telling me. My mind's racing and all these bad things are running around in my head telling me you are going me out!"

"There's an old saying, you can cut me short but don't cut me out. I've never cut out one my partners or shorted them of anything we got."

Marvin wondered if he should mention the money and jewelry, he mailed to himself. He decided to make it up to Rocky without telling him.

Rocky looked around the room and saw the manilla envelopes and stamps. "I'll bet they were going to mail the loot to someone. There's a mailbox right outside. I think some the loot must be in there."

I'd better get rid of those manila envelopes before the captain and investigators come, Marvin thought, *If Rocky can figure that out about mailing the loot they will too. Let's get rid of all the envelopes and stamps*"

"Let's not complicate the investigation," Rocky said. "Let's get rid of the stamps and envelopes. Let's go ahead and wipe the crime scene clean. I've got my eye on that gold diamond ring on the bed for myself. If there's anything you want, help yourself. We can put it in an envelope and mail it to ourselves. We've got only ten minutes to do our shopping. Here, take half the envelope from the desk and fill it with whatever you want. Then we'll mail the envelopes and call for backup."

Marvin and Rocky filled up ten envelopes each, stuffing them with money and jewelry. Then Rocky took them down to be mailed.

Rocky came back and said, "We just became rich like the Rockefellers. Remember, this is the last time we'll ever talk about what happened today. If you ever bring this up, I'll start talking about growing tomatoes. Got it? This never happened!"

"I agree, it never happened," Marvin agreed.

"Remember our story for the investigator. Let's call for backup." Rocky went down to the unmarked car and screamed for backup into the radio! He could have won an Academy Award for his performance of a panicked officer needing immediate help at the scene of a shooting!

"Shots fired! Shots fired! Fiftieth Navy Street! Officers need help!" Rocky screamed.

Within seconds, Rocky heard police sirens start wailing all around them. He kept his detective shield in one hand and his gun in the other to make sure the responders identified him as an officer and wouldn't accidently shoot him and take him for a criminal.

The first car arrived, and two officers ran out with their guns drawn.

Rocky held up his shield. "My partner, Super Jew, just took down the three robbers who killed the bank security guard. He's in the room number 12 with the robbers. I think they're all dead!"

"Rocky, are you, all right?" one of the responding officers shouted.

"I think so," Rocky called back.

A minute later, the street in front of the block was full of police cars. All the officers piled out with their guns ready.

The police lieutenant and sergeant approached Rocky.

"How did you know they were the bank robbers?" the lieutenant asked.

"They had the loot on the bed," Rocky said. "We got a tip they were here."

"You might not know it, Rocky, but they got into the vault and looted the safety deposit boxes. Nobody knows exactly what they took, because the people who hid cash in those safety deposit boxes won't report it to the IRS. If there was more than ten grand of unreported cash in those safety deposit boxes, as you know it's against the law.

"you mean the victims can't report their losses. What a shame" Rocky said.

The lieutenant and sergeant ran up the stairs, followed by officers to make sure the investigation went well.

The lieutenant looked around the apartment and got on his portable radio to tell the dispatcher to send the on-duty captain to the scene. We also need the crime scene unit. We have three bank robbers down. The arrest was made by detective Super Jew of the Twenty-first Precinct."

The lieutenant looked at the officers milling around. "Don't touch anything. Leave the room and wait outside."

The ambulance attendant arrived, and the lieutenant ordered the others to let them through. The attendants checked the pulse of all three robbers they were pronounced dead.

Meanwhile, the lieutenant interview Rocky and Marvin and took notes for the police report. When Marvin came to the story of how he shot the three robbers with guns in both hands, the lieutenant stopped writing.

"Why did you shoot them with the robbers gun?" he asked.

"I used their gun, because bullets aren't cheap."

The room broke out in laughter!

"Super Jew, I got it," the lieutenant said. "You picked up the robber's gun in your right hand and didn't have time to switch to the service revolver in your left hand, so you used their own gun to stop them before they could killed you."

"I've got more than enough evidence and statements to justify the shooting. You're both in the clear. I'll give the UF 49 shooting report to the duty captain. Do you want to visit the hospital and be examined? If not, you can have the next two days off. That's the department rule after you shoot someone. I'll take care of

of investigation. Your off duty, so go home."

They thanked the lieutenant and the officers who came to help them, then they left.

CHAPTER SEVENTEEN

We Are Rich!

In the car on the way to Rocky's house, he said, "Let's talk about growing tomatoes in case the radio's on. We'll talk more at my house."

"Not talking about what happened will be the hardest thing I've done today, "Marvin joked.

They laughed.

They arrived late at Rocky's house. He kissed his wife and said, "Honey I can't tell you what happened tonight. The less you know, the better off you'll be."

"Not another secret, Rocky, Ok. I'll leave you two alone, but please don't wake up our guests."

"I have the best wife in the world. She never asks questions. She can't get into trouble that way."

Marvin and Rocky went down to the basement and opened the door. Inside they found twenty-one king-sized pillowcases filled with cash. The clothes dryer and washing machine were full of pillowcases too, and cash spilled out onto the floor from some of the bags.

"Holy shit," Marvin said. "There must be millions here!"

"I'd guess there's over two million dollars here," Rocky said, excited. "Let's start counting."

"Right, let's get to work."

"I'll be satisfied with half of twenty-one pillowcases. We don't have to count them. Do you want to just split this down the middle? You take ten and I'll take ten. We can divide the odd one between us, so then we won't have to count all of them."

"I never thought I wouldn't give a dam about how much money I made, but I really don't care. How about you keep the extra pillowcase, and then we don't have to count any of this, and I can go home and get some sleep!" Marvin suggested.

They agreed.

"Let's meet for lunch in Sheepshead Bay on Emmons Avenue," Rocky said. "How about eleven in the morning?"

"You've got a date. We'll compare notes then."

With Rocky's help, Marvin dragged ten heavy money-laden pillowcases up the stairs and to the unmarked police car. He drove home with the piles of stuff pillowcases fill with cash in the backseat and trunk of his car.

CHAPTER EIGHTEEN

Mom, Guess What I have?

Marvin parked the car in front of a fire hydrant and opened the back door of his car to retrieve six bags of money from the back seat. He dragged them to the elevator, hoping he would not encounter any neighbors. The last thing he would need is to be stop by a nosy neighbor that would ask questions.

He opened the apartment door and knew his mother was asleep, so the tiptoed into his room and set the pillowcases in his closet. He went down on the elevator for the last four pillowcases and met Al Kane a neighbor in the building with his dog a German shepherd named Bernie,

"I saw you on the news, Marvin," Al said. "I'm so proud of what you did. I can't believe you took the police job, that is so dangerous and pays such low wages and makes you work holidays and midnight tours."

"Thanks for the encouragement, Al. You're right, police pay sucks, but the benefits make up for it. I feel like I became a millionaire when I got that job!"

When the elevator stopped at the lobby, they got out and said good-bye. Marvin opened the door for Al and make sure the coast was clear before he took the last four pillowcases from the trunk. He got back to his apartment and added them to the pile in his closet.

Staring at them, he took one out one pillowcase filled with money and dumped it on his bed. The pile of cash shocked him.

Can this be real? He wondered. *Am I rich?*

He started counting, in less than thirty minutes, the total was $129,000 and that was only 10% of the cash on the bed. He did a mental calculation and realized there was probably over two million dollars in all ten pillowcases.

Where and what will I do with all this money? Where can I store it? He sighed. *Everyone should have this problem. I'll put it back in the closet and get a good night's sleep.*

CHAPTER NINETEEN

Mom, I Have Some Good News for You

Marvin woke at eight o'clock and went into the kitchen, where Edith was drinking coffee at the table.

"Good morning, Ma," he said jovially.

"Marvin, I haven't seen you for two days, and I was worried sick about you!"

She said angrily. "you have to call me and tell me you're OK."

"I promise I'll call you. I have something to tell you, and you must promise to keep it a secret."

"You know I'm always here for you. No matter what you've done, wherever you tell me is a secret. I am always there for you."

"I know, but what I'm going to show you will be a shock to you."

"Are you in trouble?" she asked in a worried voice, "You have an uncle who's a great lawyer. I'll call him for you."

"No, I'm not in trouble. I've got good news. We're rich! Anything you want, you can have, but don't ask how I got the money. I'll just tell you that it was from people who were hiding the money and not paying taxes on it."

He took her to his room and opened the closet. Removing one pillowcase, he dumped the contents out on the bed.

Edith stared at the pile of money. "Marvin, that's the most money I ever saw in my life!"

"There's more than two million dollars in those pillowcases, Mom," he said excitedly.

Edith was stunned. "Marvin, I'll never leave the apartment. I'll keep the door locked, and we'll take turns guarding the money."

"There's more coming, Mom. It'll arrive by US mail. At least sixteen manila envelopes will be delivered by our good friend Greg postman in the next three days. Make sure you pick up the mail if I'm not here and don't forget to give Greg a big tip."

"Why don't you quit your police job? You don't need it anymore, and it would make me so happy." Edith said quickly.

"I'm having too much fun. I need to stay on the job for at least another six months to a year in the department, until things die down. Someone in the department might put two and two together and figure out I got a lot money somewhere. Nobody quits the New York City Police Department without a good reason. I promise you on Dad's grave that the first chance I get to leave the job, I will. I don't need the money or the risk anymore." Marvin chuckled.

"Maybe I've gotten older and wiser in the last two weeks, but I've done more in two weeks that most people do in their entire lives. Just go on with your normal routine. If someone steals our money, I know what to do and I'll take care of them." added Marvin.

"I have to meet someone at eleven o'clock in the morning. I have an idea what and where we can keep the money."

"I'll still stay home to guard it until your plan is worked out, Marvin, I also have a list of people who called you." Edith replied. They went back to the kitchen, where she handed him a piece of paper with a list of names and telephone numbers on it. He looked down the list for a moment.

"I'll call them back later in the day."

They sat down for breakfast and talked about their future, now that they had plenty of money.

CHAPTER TWENTY

Marvin Meets Rocky at the Diner

Marvin, arrived at the diner early, and waited in the unmarked police car for Rocky to arrive. He pulled up at eleven exactly in his ten-year-old Chevy that looked like it came from the junkyard. Rocky saw Marvin's car and parked beside him.

"Hi, Super Jew." Rocky said, "Did you sleep well last night?"

"I slept like a millionaire." Marvin said smiling broadly.

They laughed.

"Let's get out and have a talk on the fishing pier down the street."

"OK."

As they walked, they discussed what to do with the money and where they might hide it.

"I could have an answer," Rocky said. "I have a friend in the diamond district who handles a lot of money for people who have the same problem we do. They buy packets of sealed diamonds worth one million U.S. dollars each. If we buy diamond packets, we can take them to any exchange in the world and exchange them for one million cash in any currency. The fee is three percent, which isn't negotiable. So, for about sixty grand, our problems are solved. My friend can also open bank accounts in Czechoslovakia and the Cayman Islands.

"What's his name?"

"I can't tell you until you agree you're in."

"Can we trust him? What will we do with a packet of diamonds worth a million dollars?"

"I have that solved too. The most-secret, secure banks in the world are in Czechoslovakia. They're behind the Iron Curtain and our government doesn't have any relationship with them. When we want money, they transfer funds by wire to our bank in the Cayman Islands, and those banks have offices in New York City. The Czech banks have a stellar record of keeping track of every penny of their depositor's money." Rocky stated.

"Plus, get his! When we deposit over one million US dollars in their banks, it's called a jumbo account, and it pays a higher interest rate. We'll get eight percent a year, which adds up to $160,000 each year!" Rocky added.

"I think I could live on that," Marvin said jovially. "It might be a little tight, but I could manage. Let's do it. Where should meet your friend its in the diamond district as soon as possible. I have a friend on Wall Street," Rocky warned. "They're too regulated by the government. That is the quickest way to get caught. I made an appointment for tomorrow afternoon. Here's the address. It's on Forty-Seventh Street off Sixth Avenue. Don't bring any money until we reach an agreement.

"You should keep some of it at home. Don't send it all to the Czech bank. I'm keeping at least half a million here in case things don't work out."

"How do we get the diamonds to Czechoslovakia?" asked Marvin.

"My friend knows how to do that, too. He will hire a bonded diamond courier who'll carry our diamond packets to the Czech bank and will deposit the two million into our accounts. His fee isn't much, only $5,000 each. So, for about seventy thousand, our problems are solved."

"I'm on board."

They shook hands to seal the deal.

"Let's go grab lunch at the diner. I'll pay." Rocky grinned.

"Sure, you can afford it? It might be three dollars." Marvin cackled.

They laughed.

Marvin and Rocky ate lunch and joked around, but they were careful not to mention their new plans in public.

After they ate, they shook hands.

"See you tomorrow at noon," Rocky said,

'I'll be there." Marvin nodded and left for his car, as Rocky paid for their meals.

CHAPTER TWENTY-ONE

Back Home to Make Telephone Calls

Marvin met his mother in the kitchen.

"How'd the meeting go?" she asked.

"I think we straightened out what to do with the money. We're going to buy packets of diamonds each worth millions of dollar. They're easy to transport and exempt from reporting to the U.S. government. They'll be sent to Czechoslovakian banks. It will go there first, then we'll have checking accounts created in a bank in the Cayman Islands. I'll give you the account numbers in case something happens to me. It's a win-win situation. It's done all the time by people hiding cash from the government." Marvin explained.

"You aren't serious about putting your money in a Czechoslovakian bank, are you?"

"There's no way we can keep all this money in the apartment, Ma. I already made the deal. Let's drop the subject."

"Ok, here's a list of the calls you need to make," She handed him a long list from a pad of paper.

Marvin began calling, starting with Cindy.

"Hello, Super Jew," Cindy said. "You're the talk of the newsroom. Are you OK? We've been running the story of how you and your partner apprehended those bank robbers and recovered all that money! You're my hero!"

"Cindy, thanks for the complement. I just want to remind you we're going to Truman Capote's Black-and-White party at the Plaza on Saturday. When you get off work tonight, let's meet for a drink."

"Sure, how about P.J. Clark's on Third Avenue at eight?"

"I'll be there, love you."

Marvin hung up and called Truman Capote next. After he heard Truman's message, he left his own message. "I got your message. I'll be attending your Black-and-White party at the Plaza Hotel with my date Cindy. See you there."

He made several more calls and then told Edith he wanted to take a nap. "Don't wake me up until six o'clock. I want to watch the news and see if I'm on it."

·············

Edith woke Marvin at 5:50 PM, so they could watch the NBC news. Marvin sat on the living room couch, where his mother already had a glass of orange juice waiting on the coffee table for him.

As the new began, he saw Cindy working the anchor desk with her partner. The lead story was about Rocky and Marvin recovering money from the robbery and Marvin shooting the three robbers with the robber's own guns.

Marvin's comment, "He shot the robbers with their own guns because bullets aren't cheap," was quoted by Cindy. Edith burst out laughing. Then Cindy reported that over $7 million was recovered, and some people had a lot of explaining to do for hiding their money from the IRS.

Maybe we should have filled up more pillowcases, Marvin thought.

"Now I know where you got that money," Edith said. "It's the perfect crime. Those people don't dare report their missing money, because they'd have to explain it to the IRS. The bank doesn't have any idea how much is missing either.

"You're right again. You should be a detective, Ma. You're my partner in this. Anything you want, you can get."

"We'll start spending when the time is right. Let's lay low for a while. If you want, I'll go to the meeting with you to cover your back," added Edith.

"Ma, I know if you come along, we won't get gypped, and our money will be safe. The meeting's at noon in the Diamond Center on Forty-Seventh Street

"Ok, let's go together. Maybe we can pick up a diamond for Cindy?"

"I have the diamond and gold rings coming in sixteen manilla envelopes any day now. We may find one in there she would like," suggested Marvin.

"Looks like you've got all the bases covered." Edith

CHAPTER TWENTY-TWO

Meeting Cindy at P.J. Clarke's

P.J. Clarke's bar, established in 1884, was one of the oldest bars in the city. It was where Jackie Kennedy and her children, Frank Sinatra, Nat King Cole, and most of the Broadway and Hollywood stars went. It was famous for its Cadillac burgers.

When Marvin met Cindy, he hugged and kissed her, which she returned enthusiastically. They were escorted to a table in the back of the room.

"I miss you, Super Jew," Cindy said softly." You have had some two days. You have to tell me all about them."

"I had to do what I did out of fear for my life. One of the robbers opened fire on me. I must be the luckiest cop in the world because he missed! I didn't even aim my guns. I just emptied them. God must have been on my side. They missed me, but I managed to shoot all three of them!" Marvin exclaimed.

"Thank God they missed."

"I've made a decision. I plan to quit the New York City Police Department, because it's only a matter of time before I get killed. I'll miss the job, it's fun, but I'd be better off starting a business." Marvin said.

"I agree. The way you're going, it's like going 100 miles per hour in a school zone. What will you live on until your business starts making a profit?"

Marvin decided to make up a story, then he realized he had a story already in his family that was true.

"I don't need money," he said. "My family patented the shoebox in the 1800's. We receive royalties on the patent. I have enough money coming in that I don't have to work.

"You're full of surprises. When will you quit the department?" Cindy asked.

"They need me with all the riots and chaos going on. When things calm down, I'll quit."

"I'd quit now," Cindy said.

'You're right, but I have to finish a couple of things I'm doing on the job."

Their drinks arrived.

"Let's order some food and a couple more drinks. I have important business to take care of tomorrow," added Marvin.

Later they went to Cindy's apartment, where Marvin spent most of the night making passionate love to Cindy.

•••••••••••

The next morning Edith and Marvin drove to the heart of the Diamond Center on Forty-Seventh Street between Fifth and Sixth Avenues. It was the world's largest shopping center for diamonds and jewelry, showcasing over 2,660 small diamonds stores and most of the stores were booths. The booths are located on the ground floor of the buildings. There are hundreds of diamonds and jewelry booths in rows next to each other that took up the whole ground floor of the large building. Over ninety percent of the diamonds that entered the U.S. came through the diamond district, but Russian mob a criminal element tried to take over and shake-down the owner's for the money that the diamond district earned.

Marvin parked one block away from the area. He and Edith walked through and saw various jewelry store windows with rows of diamonds and other jewelry. Each jeweler tried to entice them to enter their booth and shop. As they walked to the back, a uniformed security guard stopped them.

As they enter the jewelry store for their appointment, they were stop by the big, strong security guard. "This is as far as you can go. This a secured area unless you have an appointment," stated the Security Guard.

"We have an appointment to see Morris, and these are the directions he gave me." Marvin said. "I'm supposed to go where the vault is, and his office is next door."

"What's your name? I'll see if Morris wants to see you."

"Tell Morris I'm Rocky's friend. He'll know who I am."

The guard left and returned within a minute. "You should've told me you're a New York cop. Morris and Rocky are waiting for you, follow me."

Marvin and Edith followed the guard into a large vault, that was Morris office. He had a desk with a large scale on it.

Rocky was surprised to see Edith and asked, "What the hell is she doing here?"

Before Marvin could reply, Edith interjects, "I'm here to make sure everything is kosher, and nobody gets taken advantage of."

They were taken aback by Edith's bold statement.

Morris sat behind the desk, while Rocky sat in front in a large brown leather chair. Marvin and Edith sat in two other chairs to face the desk beside Rocky. Marvin immediately saw that Morris was a Hasidic rabbi. He wore a three-quarter black Prince Albert frock coat, a traditional black hat, and side locks of hair along the side of his face.

"Edith, nobody will take advantage of your son and Rocky," Morris answers. "You have my word on that. This is what I've done so far. I already opened two secret bank account in Czechoslovakia and the Cayman Islands for Rocky and Marvin. They're waiting for the diamond packets to be deposited. If we agree to the terms of my commission, the next step is for my armed security guard to pick up your money. He'll bring it here, and we'll count it in front of you using our cash-counting machine. I'll give you Czech bank receipts with your account numbers on them. Your money is then secured, and you'll have complete access to it. It's that simple. I do this all the time."

"Rabbi, how much is you commission!" Edith asked.

"It's a standard three percent, plus a ten-thousand-dollar fee for the armed diamond couriers."

"You and Rocky can do better that that," Edith told the two men. "You'll be paying about seventy thousand for his fee. How about you give us a discount?"

"What will you do with all that money?" Morris asked loudly. "You need me!"

Marvin and Rocky stared at Edith.

"I have plenty of hiding places," she replied. "What we could do is spend the money."

Morris fought to contain his anger. "I've been doing this a long time, and this is the first time anyone negotiated my fee! You're one strong woman! Ok, how about 2.5% fee instead?"

"How about a straight fifty grand," Edith added.

"I'll give Super Jew and Rocky a police discount. Edith, it's a deal for fifty thousand."

"This also includes the courier fee. One other thing, how about you give us some collateral to hold? We'll keep a packet of diamonds worth one million each until the bank accounts are accessible."

"Edith, you're killing me!" Morris responds. "All right. We'll give you one-million-dollar packets of diamonds to hold and we'll keep the bank account numbers secret until you return the packet of diamonds. Is that a deal? Edith, we'll do the entire transaction for fifty thousand."

Edith looked at Marvin and Rocky, both of whom seemed ready to have heart attacks and asked, "What do you think?"

"Let's take it!" they said together.

They shook hands and set a date for the armed couriers to arrive to pick up the cash. Marvin and Rocky would ride back with them to the office to witness the counting of the money.

"Be prepared to spend all day and night. It's a real pain in the ass to run that much money through the cash counting machine." Morris said.

"Everybody should have that problem!" laughed Marvin and Rocky.

Morris called his assistant, who came in with a large bottle of champagne and four glasses on a gold serving tray. All four of them toasted the good life! When they finished their champagne and left.

• • • • • • • • • • •

While they were driving toward home, Edith said, "Look guys, I think we should keep at least five-hundred-thousand in cash for investing in a cash business that could be used as a front to launder the money. We'd make more money that way, too."

"What kind of business?" Marvin asked.

"I'm out," Rocky said. "I plan to retire from the department in less than a year and move to Florida. I'll buy a mansion on the water with a dock and a yacht and sail around the world."

"Ok Rocky, you're out of the business," Edith said. "But you'll have a hard time explaining where you got your money."

"Rocky, think about what she's saying," Marvin added.

"Count me out," Rocky said. "I want to enjoy my life. Look, Super Jew, after we get everything set, we'll go our separate ways. I like you, but I think your mother will take charge. I'll end up working for her."

"I don't need your advice, Edith," Rocky said. "We're a team until our money is in the bank. Then I wish you and Super Jew a good life, but you'll never hear from me again."

"You're making a mistake," Edith warned.

It's my life, and this what I want to do!" he snapped back.

They dropped Rocky at his home and agreed to see him in the morning.

CHAPTER TWENTY-THREE

Moving Day

At ten o'clock the following morning, three moving men knocked on Marvin's door. One was an armed security guard.

"Super Jew," the guard said. "Morris sent us. We're here for you-know-what."

"I have my mother here. She'll watch you load the boxes. I'll come with you in the moving truck."

"You don't mind if we search you after the truck is loaded?" Edith asked.

"Do whatever you want, the guard said. "You're the boss."

Marvin took the three men into the bedroom, where they quickly assembled boxes and wrote *Super Jew* on the side with a magic marker, adding a number to each one.

"Why are you doing that?" Edith asked.

"So, we don't mix your boxes up with Rocky's boxes," he guard replied.

"Ma, this can't be real. I make $5,500 a year and now I can afford to buy a big house in a good neighborhood that cost around sixteen thousand dollars. Gasoline is twenty-eight cents a gallon. We could live like kings just on the interest."

It took half an hour to load the truck with Marvin's boxes. Marvin and Edith noticed that movers set up a new couch and furniture beside the moving van on the street. That made it look like they were really moving someone in the building. It was clear Morris knew his business.

CHAPTER TWENTY-FOUR

Rocky's House

As Marvin and Edith rode in the truck cab with the three movers, no one spoke. Morris trained his people not to ask questions.

Rocky was on his porch swing, waiting for them when they arrived. He walked over to the curb and opened the truck door so Marvin and Edith could get out.

"Thanks for calling when you left you place," he told them. "I've been on pins and needles waiting for you. This is the biggest day of my life!"

"Let's not make a big deal over it," Edith commented. "Don't let your emotions get the better of you. We have to concentrate and not make any mistakes."

"How do you live with her?" Rocky asked angrily. "What a demanding bitch!"

"That's not a nice thing to say about my mother," Marvin said.

"Let's get this over with, so I don't have to deal with either of you again." "That's fine with me," Edith said.

As they walked into the house, Rocky stopped. "Super Jew, you and your Mother aren't invited into my house. From now on we're separate in this deal. I'll tell Morris I'm on my own and will make my own decisions. You can wait in the truck and watch as they load it with my boxes."

Rocky and the three movers went inside. They came out twenty minutes later with one less box than Marvin had.

Edith noticed the discrepancy and wondered if Marvin had more money than Rocky. She pulled Marvin aside. "Did you count his boxes?"

"Yes, we've got one more box than he does," Marvin whispered.

"Should we tell him?" Edith questioned.

"If he wasn't such a schmuck, I would, but since he wants to be a schmuck, we'll keep it to ourselves."

They rode in the truck again without speaking to each other. Rocky was angry, and the tension made the ride almost unbearable. When they parked in front of Morris' business, Rocky, Marvin and Edith got out to meet him.

"Let them unload the truck," Morris instructed. "You come into my office."

"Morris, my boxes were loaded last and are in the back," Rocky responded. "I want you to count my boxes first."

Trying to be nice, Marvin said, "Why not count the boxes together?"

"I want him to know I don't want anything to do with you and your mother. I'll make my decisions without either of you interfering."

"Let's stop the schoolyard stuff." Morris countered.

"Morris," Edith said, "If this is what he wants, that's what he'll get. We'll wait at the truck until you finish county Rocky's money inside."

"Are you good with that?" Morris asked Rocky.

"Absolutely!" Rocky smirked.

Morris turned to the men and ordered them to unload just Rocky's boxes. Marvin and Edith stood outside the truck with the armed guard, as they waited.

•••••••••••

It was five o'clock and rush hour when Morris and Rocky came back outside. The two men shook hands and patted each other's back.

Rocky turned to Marvin and Edith. "I never want to speak to either of you again. Super Jew, when you see me in the precinct, don't talk to me. Got it?"

Edith butted in, "I wish you the best. Have an enjoyable life. Good-bye."

Rocky, ignoring them walked down Forty-Seventh Street to the train that would take him home.

Morris turned to Marvin and Edith, "You're next. Let's get this truck unloaded. The movers will bring the sealed boxes to my office. Super Jew, if you want, you can stay with the movers and watch them bring out the boxes. Edith can come into my office and watch the boxes until all the money is counted. They'll never be out of your sight."

"Marvin, I'll be right back," Edith said. "Don't leave the truck." Then she checked to see if there were any obstructions to the view of the office, and she walked the route the boxes would take.

She returned a moment later. "I want you to follow the boxes to the turn in the long hallway and look out the window at the truck"

"Ok, Ma. I see the turn. The boxes will be in a blind spot."

"That's fine with me," Morris said, nodding to the movers to start moving.

Edith went inside with Morris and took her place at the door to his office so she could observe the hallway.

After the last boxes were loaded onto dollies, Marvin asked the movers to stop. He wanted to inspect the truck for more boxes, just to be sure none were left behind. Then he followed the last load into Morris' office.

"Ok, Morris said. "That was hard part,

is easy." He looked at the movers. "Go back to the truck and resume your deliveries." He handed each man a $100 tip." If we need you, we'll be in touch."

The movers left, and the armed security guard who helped to load and unload stayed to help count the cash. Morris turned to Edith and Marvin. "I have four cash-counting machines that are amazingly fast. They are the same ones the big banks use. We should be done in about three hours. Let's get going."

The armed guard cut open the large cardboard boxes, and dumped money onto a long table used for meetings. Most of the U.S. bills were $10,000 notes and stacks of bearer bonds.

They froze, staring at the pile in silence. No one expected to see such large bills or bonds. The $10,000 note was issued in the U.S. in 1934 after the gold standard was repealed. It was used for large transactions. On the note was portrait of Salmon P. Chase, the Secretary of the Treasury from 1861-1864.

"Holy shit! "Morris exclaimed. "There are stacks of bearer bonds!"

Bearer bonds were issued by businesses and the government, and there was no record of their owners. Whoever held the bond owed it and could cash it at any bank.

Marvin turned to Edith in amazement, "Can you believe this? It seems like Monopoly money!"

"Marvin, I think we hit the jackpot! There must be ten million in this box alone," she said softly with a shocked look on her face.

"You won't believe this, but all Rocky had was fives, tens and twenties. There was nothing over a hundred-dollar bill. His total was $1,841,000."

Morris shook his head. "This will take a lot longer to count. The machines aren't made to count $10,000 notes and bearer bonds. We must separate them from the other bills.

All four sat at the long table and began separating the bills. After opening the boxes and separating the $10,000 notes, the total was sixteen million dollars.

"This is the most money I ever had to deal with," Morris said shaking his head. I'll be charging you a lot more for this."

Edith looked at Marvin, who was still stunned. He couldn't comprehend the amount of money they just counted!

Edith felt she'd better take charge of the situation, "Let's see the grand total with the Bearer bonds and then we can make a deal. Part of the deal is that nobody tells that schmuck Rocky on how much money we got,"

"I have to be fair with you and Super Jew," Morris said. "How about three percent of the cash as the commission."

"That would be about $420,000 on sixteen million alone," Edith said. "That's a lot."

"If we tell Rocky about this, it won't go over well. The deal's three percent take it or leave it. To sweeten the deal, I promise Rocky will never find out how much you ended up with."

Edith looked at Marvin, but he did not respond. She turned back to Morris, "It's a deal, but let's make it a straight $400,000."

"Ok, you strike a hard bargain, Edith," Morris said confidently. "We'll take the $400,000 out what's still on the floor, and you can have whatever is left."

"What about the packet of diamonds we were going to hold until the paperwork's done for the bank accounts?" Edith asked.

"Let me run this by you," Morris said. "What will you do with the ten-grand bank notes. Wipe your ass with them? If you or Super Jew went to any bank, they would report you to the feds in seconds. The deal's off for holding the packet of diamonds as collateral. I use those packets for my business, and I'd be losing money if I gave them to you. You're going to have to trust me. Look, the cash still on the floor should amount to over a million."

Edith realized she didn't have any bargaining power. "I feel extremely uncomfortable trusting anyone with that much cash and Bearer bonds. However, we have an ace in the hole."

"What's that?" asked Morris.

"Marvin's a New York City detective. He can shut down your damn operation."

Morris considered that, "All right, you can have ten diamond packets as collateral. Edith, I hope I never meet someone like you again!"

They picked up the cash off the floor and loaded it into the counting machines. After several hours, they came up with a grand total of $19,200,080.

Morris took his commission of $400,000 in cash.

of the cash came to $2,200,800. They packed it into large shopping bags with the Gimbels label and slogan that read *Good Stuff!* On the outside. As a precaution, they double bagged the money, with newspaper on top to keep people from seeing the contents.

Marvin forgot he was rich when he said, "I think we're done; we have to carry nine shopping bags on the train home, thought."

Morris laughed, "What are you stupid, Super Jew, you're rich. You can afford a taxi! Think big from now on." He called a taxi for his clients.

Marvin went to one shopping bag, removed the newspaper covering the money, and handed the security guard a handful of money. "This is for doing a great job, thank you."

"Marvin, take it easy with our money!" Edith giggled. "Don't just give it away."

"Ma, it's the right thing to do."

Morris explained to them, "The armed diamond courier will fly to Prague tomorrow to deposit your nineteen diamond packets into a jumbo savings account. It pays 8% dividend that will be deposited into your Grand Cayman account quarterly. Every three months, you'll receive about $380,000. I hope you two can live on that. It takes two days for the diamond packets to clear, so I'll see you back here in three days. Let's meet again on Friday at ten AM."

Marvin smiled, "You've got a date."

Edith was in a good mood. After hearing how much they'd get every three months, she went to one of the Gimbel bags and gave Morris two handfuls of money. "Morris, I love you, keep the money!"

"I just want to run something by you," Morris replied. "Another part of my business is buying and selling high-end jewelry. If you have any jewelry you want to get rid of, or if you want to buy anything, come see me. I'll give you such a deal!"

I still have sixteen envelopes coming to me in the mail with jewelry in them, Marvin thought. "I might take you up on selling some jewelry."

"You're a detective and if you ever come across expensive jewelry that you want to get rid of. I'll pay the going rate for gold by weight and diamonds by clarity. We melt down the gold and take out the diamonds to make new jewelry." Morris countered.

"Morris, you have a great business," Edith said.

When the phone rang, Morris answered and learned the taxi driver was waiting for his clients in the lobby at the receptionist's desk. "They'll be right out."

"See you Friday," Marvin told Morris.

The security guard, Marvin and Edith all lifted the shopping bags and went out to the cab parked in front of the building. The driver opened trunk and the trio carefully packed the bags inside.

Marvin gave the driver their address. "Give us a good ride, and there's a five-dollar tip in it for you."

The driver looked at him in the rearview mirror. "Thanks, want me to put the heat on?"

"No," Edith said, "We're fine."

The ride home was uneventful. When they arrived, the fare was eight dollars. Marvin gave the driver two tens and said, "Keep the change."

The cabbie smiled, "Can I help with the shipping bags?"

"Yeah, that would be great."

Marvin, Edith, and the driver took the elevator up to the fourth floor with all the bags. The driver set them in from of the door and said, "Thanks for the huge tip!"

After the man left, Marvin and Edith took the bags into the living room of the apartment, closed the door behind them, locked the door. They looked at each other. "A day we will never forget!" Edith exclaimed.

CHAPTER TWENTY-FIVE

Next Day, Back to Work

Marvin awoke and joined his mother in the kitchen and found breakfast and coffee waiting for him.

"Did you sleep well last night?" she asked.

"I slept like a log, Ma. What do I need to do today?"

Edith said seriously, "I was thinking we need to invest in a business that generates a lot of cash, so we can launder the money we have. Maybe we could buy real estate in Manhattan in a good neighborhood, a multi-dwelling with a store on a busy street."

"I want you to get in touch with your cop friend in the theater district and see if he has any real-estate contacts in that area."

"You mean Smitty, the theater district cop? I'll call him when I get to work." Marvin said.

"Another thing we need is a big fireproof safe installed in one of our closets. See if you have a locksmith in the precinct. I plan to visit at least five banks today and rent the largest safe deposit boxes they have. I'll put both our names on the accounts." Edith suggested.

Marvin felt tired thinking of all they had to do He just wanted to focus on his upcoming day at work. "I'll give you carte blanche, Ma. Do whatever you think we need to do. I'll make the calls. I think buying real estate in Manhattan is a fantastic idea. How can we go wrong? It seems like we'll need at least ten safety deposit boxes."

"Let's start with five and see if we need more." Edith acknowledged.

"Ok, Ma."

After eating, Marvin dressed and ran out the door to the unmarked police car.

•••••••••••

Marvin walked into the precinct, past the lieutenant at the desk.

"Super Jew, that was some arrest you and Rocky made the other day. The captain wants to see you both in his office. He's waiting for you. Rocky is already there."

I need time to think about what I should tell the captain, Marvin thought. "I have to visit the bathroom, then I'll go to the captain's office."

Marvin went into the bathroom and looked at his reflection in the mirror. *I'm screwed.* He sat on a toilet with his mind racing. *How should I act when I get into the captain's office? I must be tough and act like a hero. I'll do my John Wayne impression. I can't mention the money. I wonder what Rocky's attitude will be toward me.*

Composing himself, he walked into the bathroom. As he entered Captain Katz office, the captain was sitting behind his desk, with Rocky sitting across from him, both were talking and laughing.

Captain Katz said, "Super Jew, have a seat. We were just talking about you!"

"I hope it was all good."

Rocky smiled and turned so he could wink at Marvin without the captain seeing it. "No, it was about you being a prick and refusing to take the money on the bed that was ours for the taking!" interjected the captain.

Marvin caught on immediately to the cover story. *If I take the fall for not taking the money, who cares? I'll still be rich!*

Marvin looked at the captain. "I was brought up that we should always do the right thing. The last thing I'd do is take money that isn't mine."

"Marvin, that money could have changed all our lives. An opportunity like that come maybe once in a cop's career, and you blew it! It's great that you apprehended the robbers. In fact, I'm putting you two up for a medal, but we'd all be better off with a couple hundred thousand dollars in our pockets. Next time you find yourself in a situation like this, I want you to call me. I'll make the right decision. We'll take care of the money first, before we make the arrests. Super Jew, I'm extremely disappointed with you, this meeting is over!"

Marvin and Rocky thanked the captain for recommending them for a medal and left the office. They stopped in the hall to talk.

"I'm sorry for how I acted toward you and you mother yesterday," Rocky said, "but I can't deal with her. Super Jew, thanks for figuring out the cover story I told the captain before you came in. I said you objected to taking the money. You should get an Academy Award for acting back there. I almost pissed in my pants when you came up with being raised to do the right thing and not taking money that's isn't yours!"

They couldn't stop laughing and patting each other on the back!

"I know my mother will forgive you. I definitely do," Marvin said. "It's over. We don't need to talk about it again."

"Just one thing," Rocky added. "I never counted my money or even looked in the pillowcases at my house before going back to the scene of the shooting. My wife had relatives staying over at our house. I tried everything to get them to leave, but they refused. I randomly went into one pillowcase and stuffed all the money I could into a suitcase. I didn't have any idea what was in

of those pillowcases. I only found out when Morris and I counted it, that I got a little over$1,800,000. I'm curious. How much money did you get?"

"Rocky, you beat me, my total was a little over $1,700,000 and I couldn't be happier with that. How much money can someone spend?"

"I feel bad that I got more money than you. Do you want to split the difference?"

"You'd do that for me?"

"Yes, will fifty thousand make us even?"

"Rocky, you don't have to do that. We're even as far as I'm concerned. Your money belongs to you. If you got more than I did, then God Bless you!"

"You're my kind of guy. I should also warn you that most of the precinct phones are tapped. Don't say anything over those phones you wouldn't want you rabbi to hear. The only way a fish is caught is when it opens its mouth. I've tapped plenty of calls, and there's no code word a criminal can use that doesn't stand out in a taped conversation, except maybe the word God."

"Think about it. Have you ever heard a taped conversation where the criminal used a word like walnut or something else that didn't make sense? You can say God almost anywhere, though and it won't stand out. If I ever talk to you and say 'God Bless you' in the conversation, drop whatever you're doing and come to my house. Remember that. I hope in sinks in because I don't want you to get caught doing something stupid. If they investigate you, they 'll be coming after me right after you."

They shook hands and left, promising never to discuss what happened at Fiftieth Navy Street again. The two walked up two flights of stairs to the detective squad's office.

The squad room office in 1968 had a three-foot-tall mahogany wood wall with a swinging wooden gate and a detective's desk beside it. The large room held twelve desks, each with a typewriter, desk light, phone and three trays to hold forms. Beside each desk was a four-drawer metal filing cabinet that could be locked. In the middle of the room was a large holding cell big enough for ten prisoners. On the wall by the steam radiator was a fingerprint Polaroid camera for fingerprinting prisoners. A long bar was attached to the wall where prisoners were cuffed while they waited to be fingerprinted. The lieutenant detective in charge of the precinct's detectives had his own private office at the end of the large room.

When Marvin and Rocky entered the squad room, they went to the blackboard on the wall and saw a message waiting for them, *Super Jew and Rocky, see the lieutenant.*

They knocked on the squad commander's door.

"Come in!" shouted the lieutenant.

The lieutenant looked angry and frustrated. When he saw Rocky and Super Jew came in, his face turned red with anger!

"Sit down, you two idiots!" he snapped. "What the hell were you thinking, Super Jew? I heard the story from the captain. I just got off the phone with him. I know you don't know shit about police work, but I put you with Rocky so he could show you the ropes. You screwed up royally! Rocky, you should have handcuffed him to a chair and called me! We could have explained the situation and all of us could have been living on easy street!"

"Lieutenant, I don't give a shit or care what you think of me and what I did, because I did the right thing by not taking that money," Marvin bellowed. "My parents and rabbi taught me stealing is wrong, I was also taught that informing is wrong, too. Whatever I see or hear stays with me."

The lieutenant, shocked my Marvin's reply, sat quietly, and waited. He regained his composure, "Super Jew, you're right. Let's pretend this conversation never happened. I'll recommend you two be promoted to second-grade detectives for the arrest of the bank robbers and killing of the bank security guard."

"One other thing, Lieutenant," Marvin replied. "I have to take my mother to the hospital Friday. Is it possible to take the morning off?"

"I also need Friday off," Rocky added, "I have to take my daughter to the doctor, and my wife can't get the day off."

"We can't give you any days off because of the riots, but I can have you fill out a UF-28, the form requesting a day off, and I'll keep it in my desk drawer. If nobody is looking for you, I'll tear it up, and you won't be charged a vacation day for time off. That's the best I can do," answered the lieutenant.

The two men thanked him for the recommendation and the day off.

"I want you two to investigate the looting at Gimbels Department Store on Fulton Street," the lieutenant said. "Take fingerprints and photos of the scene. Go through the motions to make Gimbels happy. I know it's a waste of time, at this point, and we won't make any arret from this, but it looks good."

"The vice president of the store is waiting for you to do your investigation and take down a report. I'm counting on you to make the guy happy. Get the hell out here and go see the vice-president of Gimbels, and by the way, you're partners for the foreseeable future."

"Thanks, Lieutenant," Rocky said sarcastically. "That's just what I need."

"Let's get out of here while the getting is good," Marvin said. "I'll drive."

Once they were outside the building, Marvin said, "Boy, am I glad I have Friday off, so I can see Morris an get the bank account numbers."

"We didn't need the day off," Rocky explained, "Because we would've seen him anyway. You put me on the spot! If he gave you the day off, I'd have to work with another detective to see Morris. That wouldn't work, so I had to ask for the same day off."

"I've never work with a millionaire cop before." said Marvin.

"Same here, there aren't many of us," Rocky smiled.

They laughed and got into their unmarked police car.

CHAPTER TWENTY-SIX

Gimbels Department Store

Marvin and Rocky passed police barriers and ten rookie cops who had sealed off Fulton Street, a busy Brooklyn shopping district. No civilians were in the area. It was a cleared zone for them. "Marvin said I feel sorry for all the store owners that have all their stores are closed. How can they make any money?"

"It's so stupid. It is going to take years for this business area to rebuild. Where are the rioters are hurting themselves? Where are they going to shop? Rocky said.

Marvin recognized some of the recruits from his Academy class. He drove ahead and parked in front of another group of recruits guarding the store entrance. Pete Cahill and some of the other classmates came over since they recognized Marvin.

"How's it going?" asked Marvin, as he got out of the car.

"We've been working twenty-four-hour days with barely enough to eat and little sleep," Pete complained. "We already had rookies hurt quelling the riots. Jim Healy was badly hurt with a head injury when a rioter tossed a brick off the roof. He went down bleeding everywhere. He was in a coma for three days. The doctor said he'll be partly paralyzed on his left side for

of his life."

"This is our third week on the job, and we already have five rookies quit and three hurt from our class alone. Super Jew, we heard you've become a star in the department, and already got promoted for shooting bad guys! You're the talk of the department! That was some great arrest you made of the bank robbers." I'm glad you recover all the money that the victim's loss. added Pete.

"Pete, Thanks, those skel's deserved to be killed for what they did. And there was so much money that they took. The department is still counting the money that we recovered, and that days ago. Pete, you have it a lot tougher than me with all the shit you have to deal with on the street." Marvin said.

"What are you here for, Super Jew?"

"Me and my partner, Rocky, have to prepare a robbery report from Gimbels' vice president."

"It wasn't a robbery; it was a riot! About five hundred looters broke into the place and took everything that wasn't nailed down. We were called in to make to the scene and made over fifty arrests and stop the looting!" replied Pete.

"Thanks Pete, whatever I can do you for you call me at the Twenty-First Precinct squad room."

Marvin and Rocky walked into Gimbels to meet the vice president. They entered and found the entire first floor was in shambles. Windows were shattered, jewelry counters destroyed, and the all contents of the store are gone. The entire eight story building was a wreck. Extraordinarily little escaped damage.

The vice president was waiting for them. "Glad you're here, Detectives, I have to fill out a police report, so Gimbels can be reimbursed from our insurance company for the damage done by the looters!"

"Here's my card,": This is my partner, Super Jew. We're here to help Gimbels in any way we can." Rocky told him.

"According to the officers outside," Marvin said, "About five hundred looters broke in and destroyed the place while they looted almost everthing."

"What time and day do you want us to use for the report? Rocky asked. "We can leave the report open-it's called a UF-61. When you have list of all the stolen items, give it to the Twenty-first Precinct detective squad, and we'll sign off on the report. You and Gimbels are on the honor system, so let your conscience be your guide. Whatever you want to claim with your insurance company is fine with us."

"That's the best we can do for you and for Gimbels. We'll call you and bring you a copy of the UF-61 when it's completed, then we'll file the police report with the insurance company. If Gimels had any problems with the insurance company, we'll say we investigated your report. Whatever you claim is what our investigation found." Rocky said.

"I don't know how I can thank both of you for helping us out," the vice president said as he felted relieved. "Maybe if I give each of you hundred-dollar gift certificates as a 'Thank You' that would show our appreciation. We have some genuinely nice items you can buy for a hundred dollars."

"I know," Marvin said with a smile. "Just the other day, I used your shopping bags for a job we did. Those bags are strong and hold plenty of items without breaking. Thank you for the gift certificates. That would be fine with us, but you don't have to. We're here to help you recover from your loss."

Rocky gave Marvin a look. "What about the two speeches you gave today in the captain and the lieutenant's offices about how you were raised and what the rabbi taught you?"

Marvin laughed, "That was acting."

They followed the vice president into his office. He went to his desk and took out two one-hundred-dollar Gimbels gift certificates and handed them to the detectives. "Thank you, Rocky and Super Jew."

"This investigation is over," Rocky said. "You bring down a list damaged and stolen items for the report at your convenience. We'll fill out the preliminary report and call you in a couple of hours with the UF-61 number for your insurance company."

"I'll call your precinct and tell them what a great job you guys are doing!" the vice president said.

"We'd appreciate it," Rocky replied.

They shook hands and left the store. From their car they saw Pete Cahill walking toward them. Marvin waited with the engine running until Pete reached the car.

"Super Jew, there's one thing I was thinking you could do for me," Pete told him.

"You got it, just ask."

"There's a new detail starting up, the Special Event Squad. They work from ten o'clock in the morning to six at night, it's called a scooter chart, with four days on and two off. All they do is work riots, demonstrations, parades and anything the department thinks requires a police presence."

"Sounds like a great detail," Marvin said. "It would get you away from these round-the-clock hours or riding in a car all night answering calls. I promise to call my hook in the department and see what I can do for you. Give me a couple of weeks. I'll get back to you."

"Thanks, Super Jew."

Marvin and Rocky drove away.

"Super Jew, we've got some time to kill," Rocky said. "The lieutenant thinks we'll spend all day investigating the Gimbels case. Let's get something to eat and bullshit a while."

"Where do you want to go?"

"There's a cop bar on Coney Island Avenue called the Island Lounge. It's owned by a detective in the Ninety-seventh Precinct. It's a cop hangout. Any time of the day or night you'll find women there looking for a cop to have a good time with. Believe me, some women treat cops like rock stars!"

"You've got to be kidding. Rocky, you're making it awfully hard for me to quit the department."

"I haven't told you the best part. I'll introduce you to Pat the Plumber. She hangs out at the bar and will show you how she got her name in the bathroom of the bar."

"What are we waiting for?" Marvin asked. "Let's go have some fun."

•••••••••••

Entering the dark bar, they let their eyes adjust. It was crowded for eleven in the morning. Fifty people sat at the long table around the bar. Bo, the bartender, who was an off-duty policeman, had been working the Lounge for years. He knew almost every cop on the job.

When Rocky and Marvin walked up to the bar, Bo immediately recognized Rocky. "How's it going, Rocky?" I want to give you and your partner a drink on the arm for making a great collar the other day. Is this Super Jew, the one we've been hearing about on the TV and in the papers?"

Marvin shook Bo's hand and introduced himself.

"I have one question," Bo said. "Next time you guys come across that much money sitting on a bed, give me a call! I'll tell you what to do with it. Put it this way-I wouldn't be working anymore We'd be on an island in the Caribbean drinking a pina colada."

"We didn't have a chance do anything," Rocky added quickly. "There was gunfight, and we had to call for help. Believe me, I wish we had had time to take the money, but we didn't."

"I feel for you guys. What a bummer. The chance to get rich comes once in a lifetime to a cop. Let me get you both a stiff drink. You guys need it."

Rocky and Marvin sat at the bar between two young women in knee-high boots. One wore a red minidress, and the other had a on a black minidress and a white captain's hat.

"I'd like you two ladies to meet my partner, Super Jew," Rocky said smiling. "He's new on the job and has never made love in the morning in his entire life. Super Jew, I'd like you to meet Pat and her friend Amy. They're two of my best friends. They love cops and know how to make a man happy."

Both girls were gorgeous with long, bleach blonde hair. When they stood, they were both over five-feet-ten inches tall and large breasts.

They could have any man they wanted, he thought. *Why hang out at a bar?*

"Super Jew, I saw you on TV news highlighting all the arrest you've made," Pat said in a soft, sexy voice. "I've been following you in the papers, too. You've my hero!"

"Hey Pat," Amy interrupted, "They only got an hour lunch break. We'd better see what they want to do."

Bo came over with the drinks and set them on the bar.

"We need the key to the bathroom" Rocky told him. "We're planning a party with Pat the Plumber and Amy."

He gave the key to Pat, and all four of them went to the private bathroom that was furnished like a living room with a large couch, a leather chair, and two soft pillows on the couch. It was a place where cops took their dates to make passionate love without their families knowing.

Pat took Marvin's hand and led him to the couch, pushing him down. Marvin was worried at first, then Pat started to help him remove his jacket and tie. She unbuttoned his shirt next. Marvin relaxed and became aroused. She was a knock-out for sure and one of the most gorgeous girls he'd ever seen.

Pat shoved him on this back, unbuckled his belt, and rubbed his penis until he started moaning with his eyes closed. He never experienced this before and before he knew it, she took off his pants and licked his penis. Then she blew softly and allowed himself to enjoy the best blow job of his short life. Pat enjoyed her work because she began moaning, too. Within three minutes, Marvin had an orgasm all over her face!

Pat's face showed a look of utter satisfaction. "Anything else you want to do?"

Marvin opened his eyes and saw her face covered with his sperm.

"Thanks for the best blow job I ever had! The last thing I want to do right is kiss you."

She laughed with him. "I'll clean up and meet you in the bar, so we can finish our drinks. I know you and Rocky have to get back to work."

Marvin stood and dressed. When he glances at the chair occupied by Rocky and Amy, he saw her sitting on the chair with her legs around his head as licked her. Amy's head stretched back over the chair, her eyes closed, as she screamed, "Don't stop!"

Marvin left the room and went back to the bar. He waited for Pat to meet him. When she came out with Rocky and Amy the entire bar erupted in cheers.

"Rocky, you're the man!" people shouted.

The three joined Marvin at the bar.

"That was some lunch we had!" Marvin said grinning. "How come I'm still hungry?"

They both laughed.

"I've wanted to meet you ever since I saw you on the TV news." Pat told him. "I love cops and all the hard work you do should be rewarded. I have a lot of important, high-ranking police brass boyfriends who can do a lot for my friends. If I make just one phone call, poof, whatever I ask for, is done! I'll show you. What would you like the police department to do for you?"

Marvin doubted she had that much power, but maybe she could get a transfer. He remembered Pete's request to transferred to the Special Event Squad.

"I'd like you to get my friend, Pete Cahill and me a transferred into the Special Event Squad. "

"That's all? Just a transfer? Ok, Super Jew. You've got it. When would the two of you want the transfer to go and take effect?"

"How about next Monday?" Marvin replied, but he still did not believe she had that much power in the police department.

Pat left the bar to make a call.

"Super Jew, are you crazy?" Rocky asked. "She had sex with most of the bosses in the department. She can do anything she wants. I'll bet you and Pete are both transferred by noon tomorrow."

Marvin realized he just made a mistake. "Holy shit, Rocky, I was just kidding you about going to SES."

"Super Jew, Rocky's right," Amy added. "Pat has a lot of pull in the department. Anything she asks for, she gets!"

Pat returned a moment later, "I made one call to police headquarters. You and Pete will be transferred by midnight. You will report to Traffic Unit B on Thirtieth Street at ten o'clock Monday morning. When you go back to the Twenty-first Precinct, there'll be a teletype message telling you to report to SES. Pete Cahill will get the same message."

"Wow Pat, that's impressive!" Marvin exclaimed. "Thank God I've got Friday off."

"That's another thing I did," she added. "You and Pete are off after this tour of duty until Monday."

"Let's have a going-away party drink for Super Jew!" Rocky announced, raising his glass.

Pat and Amy joined the toast.

"Super Jew,

This has been some two days," Rocky said. "Since I met you, my life has changed for the better. The best of luck to you in your new command!"

They finished their drinks. Marvin and Rocky kissed Pat and Amy's cheeks.

"We have to get back to work." Rocky declared.

CHAPTER TWENTY-SEVEN

In the Police Car

Marvin sat in the car with a big smile. "That was some lunch."

"I think you're making a big mistake," Rocky said. "You'll miss a lot of action at the Twenty-first Precinct."

"I plan to quit as soon as I can. I don't need the money anymore or the benefits the job offers."

"I'm right behind you. I've got nineteen years on the job. I'll retire in one more year."

"We don't have to take any more chances. Screw it. I'll pay for my meals. We can afford it."

"That's the problem. If we change what we're doing with all the free stuff we get on the job, we'll stand out. Believe me, someone in the department will get wise and investigate us. My advice is to play the game until we're out of here."

"You're right"

"We have to make a couple stops. I have two contracts we need to."

"What's a contract?"

"It's a deal you make with a local businessman. One contract is for us to drive the owner of the check-cashing business to the bank in our car, so he doesn't get robbed. He gives a pound each, which is five bucks apiece for the service. It takes ten minutes."

"What's the other contract?"

"That's the one that pays my bills. We have to pick up a diamond courier at Kennedy Airport and take him to the store on Adam Street. His flight lands in an hour. That earns us one hundred dollars each. For Christmas, I get five hundred dollars' worth of gifts. I have a contract with most of the jewelry stores in the precinct. This is what you'll give up by going to SES."

"Rocky, you don't need to do all that anymore. You're filthy rich."

"You're right, but it's a habit, I can't stop. I've been doing this for the last fifteen years, making contracts in the precinct."

"Ok, count me in for today. But I'm done with the contracts you made."

Rocky and Marvin fulfilled both contracts and earned an extra $105 each.

Returning to the precinct detective squad room, they went to the lieutenant's office.

"You guys did a great job at Gimbels," the lieutenant said. "The vice president called to praise the investigation you did. He said when he comes into the squad office to file the property damage report and provide a list of stolen merchandise, he'll bring $100 gift certificates for all the detectives at the precinct."

"Super Jew, I've got bad news. You've been transferred as of Monday to a detail I never heard of, but what you did for the few days you were here you could've had a good career in the detective squad. The good news is you have the next three days off. So, I tore up the UF-28 for Friday, since you are already off,"

"Lieutenant, please I still need Friday off to take my sick wife to the doctors." Rocky said.

"Ok."

"Thanks Lieutenant, for everything," Marvin said.

The two men left the Lieutenant's office.

"I'll see you Friday at Morris to get our account numbers," Rocky said when they were alone in the hall.

"I'll be there with bells on."

"Super Jew, the more I think about what you said, you're right. I don't need to stick my neck out anymore; I'm done with my contracts."

"That's the best thing I've heard all day. You just made a wise decision."

"I'll miss you," Rocky shook Super Jew's hand.

They left and signed out for the day to go home.

CHAPTER TWENTY-EIGHT

Marvin Off Duty

Marvin called Cindy at work, and she answered immediately.

"Is that you, Super Jew? I have missed you. I have been thinking about you. I'm worried that you're in danger with all the riots still going on out there!" Cindy said.

"I'm fine, and I miss you too. You are all I think about. I'm off for the next three days, and I want to see you."

"Did you forget we're going to the Truman Capote's Black-White-Party at the Plaza Hotel on Saturday? You will be introduced to the press and the partygoers as the president of the new organization called GOAL. You'll need an acceptance speech," reminded Cindy.

"I did forget about that. I must go shopping for an outfit. Could you have someone in the newsroom write the acceptance speech for me?" asked Marvin.

"I can do that for you. Let us spend the weekend together at my place in the city," Cindy said excitedly.

"I'll meet you after the eleven-o'clock news, so we can go out for a drink."

"That sounds great, see you then. Love you Super Jew." Cindy whispered.

"Love you too."

Marvin stopped at the Sydney tailor shop in the Twenty-first Precinct to pick up the two suits Sydney made for him and to see if he could find an outfit for the Black-White Party.

Seeing Sydney again, Marvin thanked him profusely for the information he provided them about the bank robbers. Then added, "Anything you need me or Rocky to do for you, you've got it!"

"I'm glad you got those bad guys, but I got the information about them from the bookmakers. They were afraid the robbers would be after them next. They are thrilled you got them out of the way. They will take care of you and Rocky on next month's pad. What can I do for you today?" Sydney asked.

I need a black-and-white outfit for Truman Capote's party Saturday,

"I have just what the doctor ordered! Sydney said, excited "I have a white tux and black vest, black top hat, and white wooden walking cane. I just have to take a few stiches here and there and it will fit you perfectly!"

"How much will I owe you?"

"Are you kidding? Nothing, it's my pleasure. Give me an hour."

"Thanks, Sydney."

Marvin went back to his car. *I have an hour to kill,* he thought. *I always wanted a Marantz stereo receiver with Bose speakers. I'll go to Crazy Eddie's Appliance Store on Kings Highway and Coney Island, since I have the money and can afford one now.*

∙∙∙∙∙∙∙∙∙∙∙∙

Marvin entered the store and approached the nearest salesperson. The salesman looked at him and asked, "Are you Super Jew?"

"Yes, I am."

"We have over a hundred televisions in this store. I saw you being interviewed on the news. How can I help you?" he asked.

"I want to buy the best stereo system you have," smiled Marvin.

The salesman took Marvin to a small room and had him sit on a leather recliner, then he turned on a Marantz 200-watt stereo receiver with Bose speakers. Marvin felt the sound from the cannons in the 1812 Overture rumbling through his chest. The sound of the orchestra was so clear, he felt like he was at a live concert!

"I'll take it," he said immediately.

"Don't you want to know how much it cost? It's a $600 system, but I can get you a police discount. We'll sell it to you at cost," the salesman replied.

"How much is that then?"

"I'll be right back. I have to check it out with the manager." He left and returned a few minutes later. "You're our hero, so he says you can have the entire system including a turntable, forget about it, for, $190 and no tax!"

"It's a deal." Marvin gave him two hundred-dollar bills. "Keep the change."

The salesman refused. "Get your car and park it in the back of the store. We'll bring you the components and your change."

Marvin pulled in behind the store. A moment later, the salesman a security guard came out with the system.

"The manager wants you to have these albums to play on your new system." He handed him the latest *Johnny Mathis* and *Beatles* records.

Marvin looked at the two album covers and thanked him. He then drove back to Sydney's tailor shop. He found Sydney waiting on another customer who was picking up an outfit for Big Mo to wear. As he listened, he realized Big Mo would be at the Truman's party too. After the customer left the store, Marvin said, "Sounds like this will be some party."

"I'm doing a good business for this cray party. I must have altered a hundred outfits in the last two weeks Let me get your two suits. I'll have you tried them on to make sure they fit properly." Sydney said.

"I'm in a rush I'll tried them on at home. I have a lot to do. I'll take the suits and tux. I know they'll fit."

"Ok, good luck!" answered Sydney.

"Thanks." Marvin took the clothing and started home.

CHAPTER TWENTY-NINE

Back Home

Marvin arrived home and parked the police car at the bus stop near the front door of his building. He carried the large boxes of the stereo system to the elevator, where he met four neighbors waiting for the elevator too.

They looked at the boxes and knew what was in them, their expressions envious They obviously wondered how a cop could afford such a thing.

"We saw a moving truck in front of the building yesterday," one neighbor said. "The men went to your apartment. Are you moving?" Another neighbor asked, "Or were they delivering something?"

"That girl I saw knocking on your door," another neighbor quickly asked, "Is she the one on NBC new?"

"Wow," Marvin said. "Nothing gets by you, does it? She was here to interview me about an arrest I made. If you must know, we got a new couch, and I just won the grand prize raffle at our synagogue-a new stereo system!"

"Marvin, you're such a nice Jewish boy," they said, getting off the elevator.

Marvin met his mother in the kitchen and told her what happened with the neighbors.

"They're very nosy people. We must be careful, none of them find out our good fortune! I was thinking we need to move to Manhattan on the Upper East Side, where people keep to themselves."

"You're right, Ma. We'll keep things low key until we move out and I quit the department."

"Here's a list of people who want you to call back. This woman, Betty, called long distance from California a dozen times. She said she's worried sick about you and plans to be in New York in the early part of June. She wants to see you. What's up with her?"

"It's a long story Ma, but I'm in love with Cindy now."

"You also have to call Big Mo, Steve Sender, and some criminal court judge who wants to be introduces at the Black-and White party, as being the Executive Director of GOAL."

"They'll shit their pants when I show up with Cindy as my date, and they announce me as the President of GOAL."

"Before you make all those calls, I have a couple ideas I want to run by you."

"Shoot!"

"We have to launder the money we've got coming in. As I said the other day, we need to invest in Manhattan real estate. With the tax laws, we could than explain all the big cash we will soon have. I'm thinking one of those new franchises, like McDonald's. Let's say we buy one and open it in Times Square in the heart of the theater district. We buy the building, with stores and rental apartments and renovate part of it into a McDonald's. We'd have no mortgage. It would be a home run. You need to call Smitty the cop and see if he knows anyone who could make a real estate deal for us at a good price?"

"I'll call him or see him tomorrow after we get the numbers of our bank accounts Ma, let me make a few calls. I promise to take care of the real estate deal tomorrow."

CHAPTER THIRTY

Telephone Calls

Marvin dialed Big Mo's number, "Hi Big Mo. It's Super Jew, I'm returning your call."

"I'm glad you called. I want you to get me and my party of eight a table at the front of the ballroom at Truman Capote's Black-and-White party. Can you do that for me?"

"Sure, if you want. I can even put you on the stage with me. I promise to get you a table in the front. Anything else?"

"I can't go on the stage because I don't want people to know I'm gay. A table at the front is fine. I must ask you a question, though. I heard you didn't take any money from the bank robber. Is that true?"

"We didn't have time to do anything but call for help. We were in a shoot-out. In just a few minutes, the captain and what felt like entire precinct arrived at the crime scene!"

"I feel for you. If you had the time, you could be rich. I could've helped you hide the money. I hope there is a next time. Thanks for getting us that table. I owe you one. Give my love to Betty, that woman from San Francisco. That I got the police car for you, so you could take her home and have a couple days off."

"You won't believe this Big Mo, but now I'm going with Cindy, the NBC news anchor."

"You're going out with Elizabeth Rockefeller? You're doing pretty well for a make-believe gay man."

"See you at the party."

Marvin hug up and called Steve Sender, who wanted to be seated in the front row beside Big Mo's table. Marvin quickly realized that where someone sat at star studded parties was a status symbol. He was getting a lot of calls from people asking him to move their groups too."

He then called the judge, who asked Marvin if he could be on the stage with the Board of GOAL, he'd like to make a speech. That was fine with Marvin. He promised the judge he'd have an opportunity for his speech.

Marvin called Truman Capote next, "Hi Truman."

"Super Jew, I've been expecting you to call. How's your love life since you became gay?"

"I never made love to so many women since you made up that story about me being gay. Knowing what I know now, I should've made that up that story myself years ago. It's a chick magnet."

"I heard you're serious about Cindy from the news. Do you know she's a Rockefeller?"

"I won't hold it against her. I hope she likes Jews."

Truman laughed, "What can I do for you?"

Marvin gave him the list of people who wanted better tables at his party and added that judge wanted to make a speech. He told Truman he would bring Cindy as his date.

"Ok, the joke's over," Truman said. "We'll make the announcement at the party that you're going straight, and you're dating Cindy. The judge will become the President of GOAL, but he'll give you credit for starting it. It was your idea!'

"Thanks Truman. It was great being gay for three weeks. Too bad I never had a gay date just to see how it would turn out."

"I'm not done with you. Someday, I'll French kiss you in front of a large crowd."

"I love teasing you."

"I'll take care of the seating arrangements. See you at the party."

Marvin hung up. He had to call Betty from San Francisco, but he wasn't sure how to handle the situation. Should he tell her he was in love with another woman, or should he say he was gay and try to get rid of her? He didn't want to hurt her. As he dialed her number, he felt uneasy.

The number she gave was the one she told Super Jew to use, her private line at work.

"Hi Betty," Marvin said. "It's Super Jew."

"I've been worried sick about you. I saw you on the national news in San Francisco. The shoot-out's, killing bank robbers and recovering all the money from the bank robbery! You're my hero!"

How can I drop her without hurting her? he wondered. "Thanks for thinking about me. Do you plan to visit New York City soon?"

"That's why I called. I'll be in Manhattan at the same hotel on June fifth. I want to get together with you when I'm in town. What's this I hear about you being gay and the President of GOAL?"

"Let me explain. People think I'm gay. My friend, Truman Capote, is gay and he bet me that he could make me appear gay to the media. We made a bet that I could start the first openly gay organization in the police department! I won, and at his Black-and-White party this weekend, he'll announce that he lost the bet and will tell the media my being gay was just a way to get GOAL started. It was fun having people think I was gay for a while."

Betty laughed, "Super Jew you're too much. How much did you win from Truman?"

"Hundreds of thousands to fund GOAL. Betty, I care a lot about you, but I have to be honest and tell I've fallen in love with someone else."

"I hope it's with a woman?"

"Yes, it is. I want to marry her and plan to propose to her soon. I'm just waiting for the right time to pop the question."

"I'll call you when I'm in New York, and we'll see if you still feel that way in June. I need to go and get home to my kids and husband. I hope to see you in June, Super Jew!"

They hung up and Marvin made a lot more calls. When he finished with the list, he was too tired to wash up and simply crawled into bed.

CHAPTER THIRTY-ONE

Bank Account Time

Marvin walked into Morris' office and found him sitting behind his desk holding a gold pen.

"I've been expecting you, Super Jew. Everything went smoothly, and your money is in the bank of Czechoslovakia. The account number is the same as your shield, 182540. Here's you deposit receipt. It looks like a phone number." He laughed.

Marvin looked at the slip and gasped, "Holy shit, it's over nineteen million dollars!"

Then Morris gives Marvin a business card and says, "this is the name of your personal banker. His name has thirteen letters, but you can call him Bud. You'll make eight percent interest. We opened a checking account for you with $400,000, so you'll have enough money to cash checks. Your checking account in the United Bank of the Cayman Islands number is 431968. You'll see your first dividend posted to that account on June 30th, then every three months afterward. You'll get $380,000 each time. You don't have to do anything in your life again, because you'll make over $1,500,500 dividends each year. Welcome to the rich and famous!"

Marvin stood in complete silence, staring at the wall. "I just realized the checking account number is the day I was appointed to the New York City Police Department. The number stands for April 3, 1968."

"Nothing gets by you, Super Jew. I'm glad you didn't bring your mother today. I think she would try to negotiate a better deal for you. One other thing-you might want some checks for your checking account, so you can start buying things."

Morris handed Super Jew a checkbook with five hundred new checks, "Just write a check for cash and go to the Cayman Island bank's local branch in person to cash it. *Never, ever* use those checks to buy or pay for anything! You don't want anyone to know you have an account there. If someone finds out about your offshore bank account, the U.S, government will be after you. They'll start an investigation, and you'd have to explain where you got all that money. Use your head! I already took out my fees, so you're set to start a new life. The most important thing for me is to get back that packet of diamonds you were holding for collateral. Then we're done."

Marvin reached into his right pocket and pulled out the sealed envelope containing the packets of diamonds. "Thanks Morris, Wow, that's all there is to becoming rich."

"Super Jew, our deal is done. If you have any problems with the account, come to me and we'll straighten it out. However, none of my clients has ever had to do that."

Marvin accepted his new checkbook and deposit slips. He shook Morris hand and said, "Give my regards to Rocky when he comes in for his account numbers."

"Don't worry, I won't tell him how much money you've got!"

Marvin left the office and went to a pay telephone on Forty-Seventh Street to call Smitty the cop at his home.

"Hi Smitty."

"How's it going, Super Jew? Every time I pick up the newspaper or watch TV, I see you! But I haven't seen you at the Four Seasons lately."

I've been busy, Smitty. I have a business proposition. I know someone who is looking for a building in Times Square with at least two stores and four rental apartments. Of course, there's money in it for you. Do you know anyone who might help me?"

"How much money are we talking about?"

"My friend said if I could find him a building for a good price, I'd get a grand. I thought of you right away. I'll split it with you. We'd each get five hundred."

"That sounds like a sweet deal. Give me a couple days, and I'll call you either way. What price range for the property?"

Marvin didn't want to pay any more than the quarterly dividend he would receive, so he said, "My friend looked at the last five building sold and came up with the price range of $175,000. That's the limit of his investment capital."

"That seems a bit low for a building in the heart of Times Square, but I'll see what I can do."

"If we find something lower than $175,000, we can split the difference between us. If you find something for $150,000, you and I could split $25,000. That's not bad for a couple of phone calls!"

"I think I just became a real-estate agent. I'll definitely call you back."

Marvin hung up.

CHAPTER THIRTY-TWO

Let's see if the Cayman Islands Bank Account Works

Marvin walked to the local branch of the United Bank of the Cayman Islands, only two blocks from the Diamond District. The building was in distinguished from those building around the bank. A passerby would never know it was a bank. He was met by an armed security guard.

"May I help you?" the guard asked.

"I have an account in the bank. I'd like to withdraw some money."

"Since this is your first time here, you have to meet with one of our vice presidents and fill out some forms. They'll take a Polaroid picture of you and also your fingerprints. Don't worry everything is held in the highest secrecy and is never shared with anyone, including the government. Please have a seat. I'll be right back once I see which vice president is available."

"Thank you. Don't you need my name?"

"No," he shook his head. "Names aren't important here. The only thing you need is your account number."

The guard left and returned a few minutes later. "Follow me."

Marvin was escorted into a plush office with a tall, slender well-dressed middle-aged blond man. As Marvin came in the man offered his hand to shake.

"I want to thank you for opening an account with us," the man said with a British accent. "This is the only time we'll ask for your name. After we fill out the necessary forms, you will need only your checking account number for future access to your account. What's your account number?"

"431968," Marvin replied.

"Let me look up your account." He left and returned a moment later with a folder. After reading something in it, he said. "Mr. Levey, you're all set. All the forms have already been filled out. Your checking account is active, and your balance is $400,000 U.S. dollars. Whenever you wish to make a deposit or withdrawal, just come in, and the security guard will escort you to a vice president's office, so he can handle your transactions in person. Our guards will also escort you anywhere you wish within a fifty-mile radius of the tristate area free of charge. Do you need an additional form to allow someone else to make a withdrawal?"

"Yes, I'd like to add my mother to the account."

"Ok, you'll have to fill out additional forms, have it notarized and signed. We frown on having anyone other than yourself do bank business." The vice president read more of the forms in the folder and said, "Your mother is already on this account."

Marvin then asked, "How does she become the beneficiary to the account?"

"God forbid anything should happen to you Mr. Levey. All she must do is bring in your death certificate and the account will be in her name only. Just so you know, your savings account in Czechoslovakia includes her name too. Is there anything else I might do for you today?"

"Yes, I'd like withdraw ten thousand dollars."

"No problem, what denomination of U.S. bills would you like?"

Marvin smiled, "Hundreds."

"Just put your checking account number on the withdrawal form and sign it. I'll be right back with your money. You can't carry that much in your pockets. Do you have a suitcase or briefcase with you?"

"I never thought of that. Do you have a shopping bag?" laughed Marvin.

The vice president smiled. "We'll give you a Gucci money bag and a set of dishes as a gift. You can use the bag any time you come to the bank."

"Thanks for the gifts."

"I'll be right back. It'll take about ten minutes to count your money and fill the bag. If you want, you can come with me to watch, or you can wait here and enjoy a glass of champagne and hors d'oeuvres.

"I trust you. I'll wait here and have a party for one!"

"I'll join you when I get back." He picked up the phone on his desk and called an assistant to bring champagne and two plates of hors d'oeuvres."

An assistant came in with the food and drinks a moment later.

"Do you need anything else, Sir?"

Marvin looked at the plate and saw it held caviar and French champagne, a Blanc de Blanc Grand Cru from Franck Bonville. *I like being rich*, he thought.

The assistant left, and the vice president returned a minute later with a box of dishes and a Gucci bag filled with hundred-dollar bills wrapped packets of one thousand.

Marvin took the bag and pulled out two of the packets of cash to double-check they were accurate. Then he stood, shook the vice president's hand, and thanked him.

"Thank you for opening an account. We're here to assist you in any way possible. Do you need help carrying the bag and dishes?"

"No thanks, I'm good." Marvin walked out of the bank and got is his police car with a huge smile.

....

Marvin walked into his apartment and found his mother waiting in the kitchen,

"How did it go today?" she asked.

He explained what happened and told her about getting in touch with Smitty for help finding a piece of property. He then told her about his experience at the bank.

"Have a look in the bag,"

She gasped, "Wow, that's an expensive set of bone china dishes."

"You ain't seen nothing yet. Look in the Gucci bag."

She almost fainted when she saw the cash. "Marvin, how much is this?'

"Only ten grand, we still have $390,000 in our checking account." Then explained the process for withdrawing money and added that she was his beneficiary on all the accounts.

"Don't talk silly, Marvin. I'll be long gone before you. I have more good news, too."

"What's that?"

"Greg the mailman arrived this morning. He hand deliver sixteen manila envelopes, because they wouldn't fit into our box. I took the liberty of looking in one of them and couldn't believe all the diamond and gold jewelry I found! I'm in shock! There must be millions of dollars' worth of jewelry. Remember when I didn't want you to become a cop? I was very wrong. You can't beat the benefits."

"I think we hit the jackpot. We have to hide those envelops and figure out what to do with the jewelry."

"I found a great hiding place. I put them in a laundry bag in the bathroom hamper."

"That will work for now. I must pick out some jewelry for Cindy to wear at the Black-and White party. She'll be the talk of the town."

"How do you plan to explain where you got jewelry worth a million bucks to Cindy?"

"I can't, that was a bad idea. I'll forget about it."

CHAPTER THIRTY-THREE

The Black-and-White Party

Marvin arrived at Cindy's apartment at six o'clock. She had just returned from the hairdresser and nail salon. Her gown hung on the door. Marvin took one look at the silk black-and-silver gown and knew it was made by a top fashion designer.

"Cindy, you're beautiful already, but I can't wait to see you in that gown! You'll be even more gorgeous! Who made it?"

"It was custom made by the world-renowned designer Mary Quant. She studied art and design at the Goldsmith College of Art in London. She also designed a gown worn by the Queen of England and many of the rich and famous women in the world. Anyone in high society will take one look at it and know immediately who designed it."

She looked at Marvin. "You look great too. Who designed your tux?"

"Sydney Fine, a tailor in the Twenty-first precinct. He designs suits for drug dealers and gamblers."

They burst out laughing!

"Super Jew kiss my cheek. I don't want to mess up my makeup. Making love is out of the question until we get back home."

"I promise not to touch you until we're back here after the party," he said disappointed. "But once I get you back her, all bets are off. I'll be all over you like a cheap suit!"

"Talk is cheap. You have a date in my bedroom later tonight! I have a limo coming for us at 6:30. I'll pay for it. I know you can't afford it on a cop's salary.

"Thanks for the offer, but I was meaning to talk to you about our money arrangement. I don't want you paying for everything. I know your rich, but I want to pay at least half."

"I *am* rich! My family is in the top two percent of the wealthiest people in the country, so don't worry about paying for the limo. I've got it."

Marvin thought fast and came up with a story. "I have a pleasant surprise for you. I'm the heir to the man who invented the shoebox. My great-grandfather invented it at the turn of the century, and my mother receives royalty checks every quarter. It is more than enough to live on. I started getting my royalty checks when I turn twenty-one. I want to go half on our expense, I can afford it."

"I'm stunned to hear you offer to pay half, but you don't have to impress me about how much money you will have. Believe me, I can support both of us. My family's worth about sixteen billion dollars. My grandfather, John Davison Rockefeller, was the richest man in the country at the age of twenty-five back in 1855. When he started Standard Oil, he parlayed it into a monopoly, then he bought real estate from coast to coast. We couldn't spend all my family's money if we wanted to. The interest I earn each quarter is enough to run a country. The funny part is, I took a job that pays only thirty thousand a year."

"You've got me beat. I make only five thousand a year as a detective with overtime. I'm certainly not as rich as a Rockefeller!"

"It's too soon to discuss, but if or when we get married, you'll have to sign a prenuptial agreement. You'll keep what's yours, and I'll keep what's mine. We'll talk about that when we get serious about our relationship!"

Holy shit, I thought I was rich. She could buy and sell me dozen times.

"If that is what you really want, we'll go half on the expenses. So, you owe me $125 for tonight's limo," Cindy added.

"I thought we'd start splitting the bills tomorrow," Marvin laughed. "Just kidding."

"Ok, have you ever walked the red carpet before?" asked Cindy.

"No, what's that?"

"Get used to it. Our limo will pull up in front of the Plaza Hotel, and a doorman dressed in a top hat and uniform will open the door, A large crowd of spectators will be lined up along the curb. TV reporters from all the major networks will interview us on live TV. Then there will be a long line of newspaper, gossip columnists, and magazine reporters who will want us to stop for pictures and more interviews. This will be the fashion highlight of the 1968 season, so it will take about an hour to get through. Remember, those reporters want to create stories to sell to their media."

"I always keep it light and funny. I have a suggestion; you could talk about GOAL. Tell them you are making a huge announcement during your speech. They'll eat it up, and you'll be the lead story on all the TV and newspapers in the country!" Cindy said slyly.

"What's the huge announcement?" Marvin asked.

"Dummy! One, you have a female date, me! Two, you were never gay, and it was a bet you made with Truman Capote to start GOAL. That you wanted to fight for the civil rights for gay police officers in the city."

They finished getting ready for the party, took the elevator and walked past the lobby desk.

"Ms. Sears, you look beautiful in that gown." The doorman said.

"Thank you, Andy," she replied.

Marvin eyed the man, "What am I, chopped liver?"

"Super Jew, you look good too, but not as good as Ms. Sears."

They all laughed.

The chauffeur jumped out of the limo and opened the rear door as they approached. It was a brand-new Cadillac, complete with a stocked bar, phone, and plush seats.

"My name is Nelson," the driver said. "Anything I can do to make your ride more comfortable, just ask. Help yourselves to the bar and the phone. Tell me if you want me to adjust the temperature. I'll be parked down the street from the Plaza the entire night, so I can return there in minutes."

"Nelson, thank you." Cindy said. "Everything is fine.

We'll have the doorman at the Plaza call you when we're ready to leave."

"I'll have a sign in the window with both your names on it, so you easily recognize the limo."

As he pulled away from the curb, Marvin opened the bar and took out two champagne glasses. "Would you like to join me in a toast to us?"

"Yes!"

Marvin poured champagne into the glasses and gave her one. "Cindy, I'm the luckiest guy in world since meeting you!"

"Super Jew, you're my hero. I love you. I think I want to spend of my life with you."

"Let's see how the party goes before I ask you to marry me."

They talked and joked, sipping champagne, as they rode through the city. Then they joined the line of limo waiting in front of the Plaza Hotel. It took twenty minutes before they were finally at the red carpet.

A doorman opened the door for them. The moment Cindy and Marvin stepped out, the crowd of over one thousand spectators shouted and took pictures. Roger Grimsby, the WABC reporter who in 1968 started the eyewitness news format, approached the couple. Behind him came a cameraman with a live TV camera. He stopped in front of the couple and held out his microphone.

"Hi, Cindy Sears," and asked, "Is this what you do on your day off from NBC News? Get interviewed by WABC?"

"I always wanted to be on WABC News," she joked. "I hear they have better benefits."

"Is Super Jew your date for the Black-and-White party tonight?"

"He and I are an item. Marvin has an important announcement to make about the new organization called GOAL, which is being created to protect gay police officers."

"Super Jew, do you want to make the announcement now to a live TV audience?" Roger asked quickly.

"I'd love to give WABC the scoop, but you'll have to wait for my speech that I am giving tonight. But I'll give you a hint. Judge Lance P. Morgan will be taking over my spot as President of GOAL."

Does that mean you're handing over you position to Judge Morgan?"

"That's right. I'll remain on the board and will do as much as I can to fight for the rights of our gay police officers."

Roger turned to the camera, "You heard it here first! Judge Lance P. Morgan will be the president of GOAL." He turned back to Marvin. "One more question. With all the riots, looting, and chaos in our city, when can we expect the riots to end?"

"I promise the citizens of New York City that the riots and chaos will be over a soon as possible. I believe the assassination of Dr. Martin Luther King has put a spotlight on civil rights and tolerance for all people, and that's a good thing. GOAL is being created to achieve civil rights and tolerance for many of our police officer that must hide their true sexually or be fired. It's crazy."

"My experience with the riots gave me the opportunity to change my life for the better. If that hadn't happened, I would never have had a chance to apprehend those bank robbers and recovery all that money for the victims or be rewarded to become a detective. I would never have met Cindy and be interviewed by you on live TV. Thank you, Roger for giving me the opportunity to vent."

Cindy and Marvin walk down the red carpet, waving to the crowd. They made twenty stops to give quick interviews along the way. Finally, they reached the end, and had their last interview with Robert O'Malley of the *London Daily Mail*.

"Cindy, who's your date tonight?"

"Super Jew, he's a New York City Police detective and president of GOAL. He's been on the news in the past three weeks for all the arrests and awards he received."

"Super Jew, we want to thank you for standing up for the rights of your fellow gay officers in the police department."

"Thank you for your support of GOAL, Mr. O'Malley. I promise to do my best to protect the rights of all minorities in the city."

Cindy nudged Marvin "We need to go now; we're running late for the party."

They went into the lobby and were directed into a large room filled with priceless works of art, which would be part of a silent auction to raise money to support GOAL.

As they studied the artwork, Marvin said, "GOAL will raise tons of money from these works of art!"

"You're right, they'll probably get enough money to lobby the government to pass legislation for gay people's rights!"

"I never thought about that. We need funds to get bills passed. Maybe we could even get a tax law that would reduce our tax burden for our organization."

"You're pretty naïve about how the government works. It won't be easy getting laws passed to reduce anyone's tax burden. You need money and the promise votes for the elected officials before anything will get done! Let's look at the artwork. We'll bid on something if we like it."

"Sure, it's going to a good cause." Marvin chuckled.

They found a beautiful oil painting by Norman Rockwell, who was born on February 3, 1894 in New York City. He was famous for painting three hundred and fourteen covers for the *Post* magazine. Cindy and Marvin loved the painting.

"Let's make a bid for this," Marvin said. "We could split it. You can keep the painting in your apartment if we win."

"That's a deal," Cindy agreed. "

They laughed.

"How much do you think it's worth?" asked Marvin.

"It's not a painting, it's an investment! We'll hold it for a couple years, and probably be able to double our money. I think it's worth around ten thousand dollars, so let's bid $10,500. If we sell it, we can split the profit. What do you think? I can pay for it now if we win the painting. If you don't have the money."

"I have the money, let's bid twelve thousand to make sure we get it. I'd like to use your name on the bid, so no one asks how I can afford to bid that much money a cops salary."

"You're making a mistake if you don't put your name on the bid. All the money is tax deductible."

Cindy filled out the forms and put their bid of $12,000 in a sealed envelope, then placed it in the box in front of the painting. They went to the bar, where she ordered a chardonnay. Marvin thought about the drink he had at Ferrell's bar and ordered a Jack and Coke.

"That's Jack Daniels and coke, right?" the bartender asked. "Do you want the select Frank Sinatra blend of Jack Daniels Tennessee Whiskey?"

"Sure."

"You're the detective they call Super Jew, aren't you? I saw you on the news. I just want to let you know that the select sells for $150 a bottle. This drink will cost you $15, that's a lot for a cop to spend."

"You're right, any cop discounts?"

"Not many cops come here, and I have a lot of family on the job, If I don't take care of you, my family and cop friends would never let me forget it. Drinks are on the arm for you and your date tonight."

"Thanks! Let me know if I can ever do anything for you, call me at the Twenty-first Detective Squad Room."

The bartender left to make their drinks.

"We just bid twelve thousand dollars for a painting, and you're bargaining for price of our drinks," Cindy said. "You must be Jewish!"

· · · · · · · · · · · ·

Entering the ballroom, they were immediately escorted to their seats at one of the front tables. Marvin said good-bye to Cindy and kissed her cheek. He walked onto the stage and took his designated seat. Cindy sat at a large, round table with Arlene Francis of the TV show *What's My Line?* And Katharine Graham, the *Washington Post* newspaper publisher, Jackie Robinson and his wife and several other movie and sports stars.

Marvin walked up to Judge Lance P. Morgan and placed his hand on the judge's shoulder. "Judge Morgan, I have something important to tell you about GOAL."

The judge looked up at him. "What's so important?"

"I plan to resign from the police department and work full time for GOAL. I met Cindy Sears and fell in love; I'm totally confused about being gay!"

"Super Jew, most of us are confused about our sexuality. If you're in love with Cindy, go ahead and marry her."

"My feelings about women are changing You're right, I might not be gay, but I'll still support the gay cause. I plan to announce my resignation tonight. With your help, we'll run GOAL together. I'd love to announce you as the new president of GOAL, what do you say?"

"I was planning to ask you for more power on the board anyway, to be able to achieve our mission. I would be my honor to become president of GOAL! Go ahead and make the announcement."

At eight o'clock the room was filled with well-dressed, powerful people from business, government, sports, television, and the movie industries. Music was provided by the New York Philharmonic and people were dancing.

Truman Capote walked up to the microphone and tapped the gravel on the podium. The orchestra stopped playing, and people turned to look at Truman. "Dinner is being served," he announced. "After dinner we will announce the winners of the silent art auction. Then there will be speeches by various people, and finally the dance floor will reopen. We will party until they throw us out of here!"

....

After dinner, Judge Lance P. Morgan went to the podium to announce the winners of the auction. When he was halfway down the list, he announced Cindy Sears had won the Norman Rockwell painting. Hearing that she was overly excited and couldn't wait to see Marvin's reaction.

After the Judge finished, Truman Capote came to the microphone and thanked Super Jew for starting GOAL. He also asked everyone in the audience to make a tax-free donation to GOAL. He then proposed a bet with Super Jew, "If we raise over one hundred thousand dollars tonight for GOAL, Super Jew you will let me French kiss you here tonight on the stage!"

"You've got a bet!" Marvin called out.

"I pledge one hundred thousand dollars to GOAL." Truman proclaimed immediately."

Marvin got up quickly form his seat and only had time to say I'm Just kidding, When Truman rush over to Marvin seat and grabbed him, stood him up and gave him a long, hard French kiss. People gasped! Instantly Marvin turned to the audience and said, "Boy, what I do for money!"

Everyone howled!

Cindy turned to her dinner companions and said, "See who I have to compete with, Truman Capote!" People at her table grinned.

....

Finally, it was Marvin's turn to address the audience. He set his prepared speech on the podium and smiled. He didn't feel nervous at all.

"My name is Marvin Levey, known as Super Jew. I'm a detective in the New York City Police Department. I want to thank all the people who helped me start our new organization, GOAL. Its purpose is to protect and defend gay police officers' rights. It's a great cause, and I'm honored to part of it, with the support of people like you we will work toward obtaining civil rights for all minorities. I would like the following people to stand and be recognized for their effort in getting this organization started. Please hold your applause until I have revealed all their names."

Marvin started with Truman Capote, then included Mayor John Lindsay, Judge Lance P. Morgan, and another twenty names in alphabetical order. When he finished, they all received a standing ovation. Marvin then shocked everyone by saying, "I am stepping down as president and chief operating officer of GOAL, and Judge Morgan will be taking my place!" Then he wondered, *Is this the right time to resign from the police department?* He decides not to. Since the mayor was in the audience, it would embarrass him and many others who support GOAL, if he told the press before he told them.

"Would Cindy Sears please come to the stage?" Marvin asked.

Surprised, Cindy hesitated then gained her composure and walked up to the stage, meeting Marvin at the podium. Marvin took both of her hands and knelt down, "Cindy, I'm in love with you and want to marry you. Will you marry me?"

Cindy blushed, "Super Jew, I love you too and want to spend of my life with you—yes!"

Marvin stood and turned to Truman Capote, "Eat your heart out!" He took Cindy in his arms and gave her a big, long kiss."

The entire ballroom erupted in applause and cheers.

Truman interrupted their kiss, "I wish you and Cindy the best, and hope you'll invite me to the wedding. Super Jew, you have distinct privilege of being the first non-gay president of GOAL. That proves GOAL does not discriminate!"

"Truman, you won the bet. Thanks for your best wishes, I want to assure you and the organization that I'll give 110% to our mission. We'll do everything we can to stop bigotry against all gay people in this city and the world."

Marvin and Cindy were leaving the stage when anti-gay protesters suddenly entered the rear of the ballroom. They shouted anti-gay slogans and held up large anti-gay signs. Before Marvin could speak into the microphone to say anything, he saw to his far right two armed anti-gay protesters with semi-automatic handguns rushing toward the stage. He grabbed Cindy and Truman and shoved them down behind the podium just as the men fire! Marvin realized he might be the only one armed and able to defend the crowd, due to New York City's gun laws being one of the toughest in the country.

Marvin saw Judge Morgan get shot in the head and fall to the floor of the stage. Judge Lance Morgan laid motionless on the stage in a pool of his blood.

Marvin took out his off-duty Smith and Wesson five-shot revolver, took aim and fired twice. One of the armed men fell to the floor, the other shot at the seated dignitaries on the stage. The anti-gay protester emptied his fifteen-shot semi-automatic and then paused to reload.

Marvin tackled the man, but he grabbed Marvin's gun, they wrestled for control of the gun! Marvin knew whoever lost the battle for his gun would die. Marvin bit into the man's right ear and ripped if off his face! He howled in pain, releasing Marvin's gun, and clutched his bloody head into both of his hands, screaming in excruciating pain. Marvin rolled to the left, aimed, and emptied his gun into the man's head!

Marvin lay on the stage, staring at the ceiling, totally exhausted. He ached all over and was covered in blood from the man he just killed. *This is the right time to quit the department*, he thought, *being a cop is too dangerous for the money you make.* Before he could move, Cindy and Truman reached Marvin.

"Super Jew, are you, all right?" Cindy screamed. "Please, God, don't let him be shot!"

"Thank you for saving my life," Truman exclaimed.

I'm quitting my job as a New York City detective," Marvin shouted, "It's too dangerous!"

Mayor Lindsay and several policemen rushed to the stage. In a shaky voice, the mayor said, "Super Jew, you are a hero for saving my life and lives of all the people in this room! Anything the City of New York can do for you, just ask."

Marvin held Cindy firmly and looked up at Mayor Lindsay, the crowd of newspaper and television reports who surrounded them, and said, "The city of New York can accept my resignation, I quit! The officers in this city don't get paid enough to risk their lives dealing with the scum and losers like this."

He reached for his empty revolver and took out his shield, handing them both to the mayor. "I'm out of here, you can shove this job up your ass! Cindy help me up. Let's get out of here."

He stood, feeling shaky on his feet.

"Super Jew, please reconsider," the mayor said. "We need people in the police force like you."

Marvin held tightly to Cindy's hand and said, "Mayor Lindsay, my mind is made up. Lying on the floor covered in blood made me reevaluate this job. Sorry, I'm not changing my mind." He looked at Cindy, "Let's go, we have a great life ahead of us."

"I love you Super Jew"

"I love you too."

They hugged and kissed, then pushed their way through the crowds and left the ballroom to start a long, happy, and beautiful life together!

THE END

www.ingramcontent.com/pod-product-compliance
Lightning Source LLC
Chambersburg PA
CBHW020631110726
47899CB00002B/735